DOG BOY

and other harrowing tales

DOG BOY
and other harrowing tales

SHORT STORIES

Erica-Lynn Huberty

[signature] 2013

i-UNIVERSE BOOK PUBLISHERS
BLOOMINGTON

Dog Boy and Other Harrowing Tales

Copyright © 2010 Erica-Lynn Huberty

All rights reserved. No part of this book may be used or reproduced by any means, graphic, electronic, or mechanical, including photocopying, recording, taping or by any information storage retrieval system without the written permission of the publisher except in the case of brief quotations embodied in critical articles and reviews.

This is a work of fiction. All of the characters, names, incidents, organizations, and dialogue in this novel are either the products of the author's imagination or are used fictitiously.

iUniverse books may be ordered through booksellers or by contacting:

iUniverse
1663 Liberty Drive
Bloomington, IN 47403
www.iuniverse.com
1-800-Authors (1-800-288-4677)

Because of the dynamic nature of the Internet, any Web addresses or links contained in this book may have changed since publication and may no longer be valid. The views expressed in this work are solely those of the author and do not necessarily reflect the views of the publisher, and the publisher hereby disclaims any responsibility for them.

The following stories have been published in a somewhat different form in the following journals or magazines:

"Dog Boy," The Minetta Review, New York, NY.
"Forever Jim," The Gallatin Review, New York, NY.
"In Blackbrooke Hall," Thirteen Stories, Nocturna Press, Vancouver, BC.

ISBN: 978-1-4502-2330-0 (pbk)
ISBN: 978-1-4502-2328-7 (cloth)
ISBN: 978-1-4502-2329-4 (ebook)

Printed in the United States of America

iUniverse rev. date: 4/20/10

For my mother, Gail Cherne Gambino,
and my grandmother, "Fifi" A. B. Cherne,
who taught me to love stories;
and for Ann Hood,
who taught me to write them.

For the most wild yet most homely narrative which I am about to pen, I neither expect nor solicit belief.

~ E. A. Poe

CONTENTS

1. *1988* . Dog Boy

2. *1940* . Counting Sheep

3. *1971* . Forever Jim

4. *1916* . In Blackbrooke Hall

5. *1883* . The Dream

6. *present day* . The Black Cat

~ 1988 ~
# Dog Boy

1.

The day Doc Emmott was tracked down and mauled by a pack of hounds, I caught my break. His face was ripped to shreds in the short time it took for us to get to him. As you may have already guessed, the commotion was enough to distract everyone, providing me and that little fuck, Freddy McGuirre, with the chance for a safe getaway. Well, *safe* probably isn't the right word, but since I was spending my days doing time in Cheyenne Pen, I figured a year in solitary was a small price to pay for a shot at freedom.

But I'm going too fast. That was only a few days ago (as hard as that is to believe). It started a little further back: 1982, fifteen years after my conviction.

2.

I came to Cheyenne in 1967, wearing a gray jumpsuit, shackles around my ankles and wrists, and a plastic ID bracelet that said "Seamus Gideon." I had been tried and convicted for murder. I suppose I did help kill a man, but I did it unintentionally. There was a factory that manufactured army combat uniforms to be shipped out with our boys to Vietnam. These uniforms would return by way of body bags, if things went the way most people thought they might, and by 1967, they were doing just that. I don't know if I'm sorry I got involved in all of it. I am sorry that an innocent person lost his life and that I wasted twenty-one years, from '67 to '88, in a Montana hell pit called Cheyenne Penitentiary.

I once read that terrorism was "the act of willfully killing an innocent to force the enemy to surrender." I didn't even know an innocent was in that factory after hours. But that does not make the crime or that theory any less real, I guess.

Andrew Polis, a college buddy of mine, had the whole thing planned. He had this girlfriend, Abigail. She had long, sable-colored hair and wide blue eyes that said she'd do just about anything for him. I was the tagalong, a mascot of sorts who supplied an ear for Polis's invectives and the grass to get through them. I definitely didn't plan on Andrew implementing something so spontaneous and destructive when he drove his car up to the building and threw a pipe bomb through the window with Abby and I in the back seat, and I am fairly certain John W. Lawrence—sweeping up some last shreds of cloth—didn't count on being blown apart that warm September evening as he put in his overtime. The next week, because I'd been taken in once before for dealing, I was arrested and charged with murder. Andrew was not, and I didn't rat on him either, though I've often imagined doing so.

Another irony in all this is that I was not, nor am I now, a man of great purpose. I did not burn flags. I did not even burn my draft card; although whether I would have gone over to Vietnam is something no one will ever know. My hair fell just below my ears, I wore jeans, and I got through two years of college, filtering myself in and out of quiet bookishness and social interaction with apparently intelligent, but sometimes misguided, students. I sold some grass and smoked probably a little too much of it. People seem to like me and I have few enemies, even now. Back then, that seemed enough. I liked being liked. But I was easily swayed, and I was, too often, idle. Looking back on it, I think the idea of Andrew acting for some greater cause than myself was appealing, but I can't pretend I wasn't horrified at how that was carried out.

I don't know of anyone else in Cheyenne with a record like mine, but it's more than likely there are at least a few vigilante war protestors out there in other states. Montana's not known for its political liberalism. It's a sprawling, beautiful state with more elk than people and more farms and gun ranges than sidewalks. California and New York might be where other retired counterculture revolutionaries still lurk—Black Panthers, SDS, and the like. Even Illinois. But not Montana. I grew up in this state, and I know seven guys in my town alone who went over to Vietnam voluntarily. One and a half came back: the half being the son of our neighbors, who was returned to his parents in a wheelchair, mute, with a sort of sweet smile stuck to his lips.

I won't kid you; prison life is a perdition. Between the child molesters and rapists, serial killers and contract hitmen, the prison population makes up a group of real model citizens. But there I was. And I did not always live on Cellblock Nine, either. Before that, it was four years on Three. By the first year, I had been cornered and beaten eight times on the exercise field and the corridors surrounding the book room, and—I'll save you the graphic description—treated to indignities twice by one of our more infamous residents, Clark Howard. He had a little gang called the Cheyenne Angels. The Angels were Howard's four two-hundred-pound henchmen, each of whom never walked without a Bible tucked in their back pockets. I was lucky. I only got it twice. Doc Emmott did not have that kind of luck at Cheyenne.

Time was going along, as it does when you're serving twenty-five-to-life, when Dr. James Patrick Emmott joined our happy family in 1977. I first saw him when he was escorted past John Longman's cell to the cell next to mine. I was living with Floyd Luther Bennet, a quiet, book-loving man who never raised an eyebrow as long as I didn't shake the top bunk when I rolled over in my sleep.

It was not until the following afternoon on the exercise field that I got a closer look at Doc Emmott, who now, I noticed, somewhat strangely resembled my old friend and revolutionary, Mr. Free-and-Clear Andrew Polis.

Emmott was standing quietly near the south end of the yard with a black eye. His spine was to the fence; I guessed he'd already found out that watching one's back is a pretty good idea at Cheyenne. I can't remember anyone else who got it as bad as Doc Emmott. Except maybe a guy from California who was in for art forgery—several million dollars' worth affecting a wealthy Montana family estate. Clark Howard took a real liking to him. Howard liked them helpless—the more of a pussy you were, the closer friends you were going to be with Clark Howard. Poor Doc didn't figure that out until years later. Eventually, he landed Howard in the infirmary with a fractured skull and a broken arm. I'd like to think Doc actually broke his arm with his bare hands, but I don't see how that was possible. The way I figure it, Howard took a mighty big fall near those heavy steel shelves in the storeroom, and I believe it's because Doc pulled one of his quick slides on him. If there was one thing about Doc Emmott, he was quick as lightning. But more about that later.

Doc Emmott, a fair-haired man with unnerving green eyes, was of average height and build who, behind wire-rimmed glasses, appeared completely unapproachable. So when I went over to the south end of the fence, I did not extend my hand. The day Emmott stood at the end of that exercise yard, he was twenty-eight years old. He was two years my junior but looked as solemn and old as a lifer near the end of his sentence.

Emmott eyed me with the stillness of a cat. The reflection of the sun on his glasses blocked his eyes. He waited for me to speak.

"Seamus Gideon," I said. My mouth managed to twitch upward in a friendly gesture. He returned it with, "James Emmott."

I nodded. We spent the remainder of the hour staring up at the top of the fence. I was imagining the potato fields beyond it, the fresh air teasing my nostrils. I thought Emmott must have been doing the same thing, though, after ten years in the pen, I knew it was a bad idea to reflect on the air outside the fence.

The next day, I followed him to his seat in the cafeteria. Lunch was served daily at noon. The meals at Cheyenne blend in my mind into one pot pie of fat and potatoes. However, I can actually recall the meal that day. Hot dogs, beans over-well, and raw greens. Emmott's plate held two buns with a heap of lettuce on top. Vegetarians do not make the most fearsome of impressions in prison. I wish I could say I felt sorry for him, but I didn't. I sat myself down next to him. He continued to eat, not looking up or to his left where I sat with four dogs and a pile of pasty well-overs.

Floyd sat across from me, his face partly hidden behind a library book. Another Dostoevsky, Floyd having made his way through Tolstoy and Chekov. Next, he would move on to the Irish—Yeats, Joyce, and the like. It was all part of his self-improvement program, beginning, of course, with the oldest book, the Bible, which he returned to nightly regardless of what other piece of literature he was reading during the day.

I laughed out loud at the sight of Floyd—in for double-homicide—reading *Crime and Punishment,* and Floyd eyed me with a deep, satisfied smile. I want to add here that I laughed, but not at Floyd. Not ever at Floyd. For all his books and his few spoken words, Floyd was six-foot-five, two hundred and seventy-odd pounds, with skin as black as coal, beneath which lay thick, smooth, rolling muscle. More than that, Floyd had a spirit that sparkled slow but steady behind his solid brown eyes. He was fair, consistent, and hard as steel. He was the reason Clark Howard and the Angels let me be. A lot of inmates came to him for advice and to settle fights, but nobody fucked with Floyd Luther Bennet.

John Longman joined the table then. He sat down next to Floyd, patted him on the back, and scraped his apple crumb onto his plate. I gathered it was a thank-you for one of Floyd's interceptions or words of wisdom.

John was a very tall Indian—a Crow—with jet-black hair that was always in a neat, shiny ponytail; a curiously jagged scar over his right eye. I was glad to see John go in '79 after the governor granted him a pardon. In for a rape and murder he vehemently denied committing, I never felt like he deserved to be there. It's extremely rare to feel that way about someone in prison. I met a lot of guys in the pen: some I liked, some I even felt sorry for, but John was the only one I ever believed was innocent to the core. Even I was culpable in my own imprudent way.

It was Freddy McGuirre who started the first conversation with Doc Emmott. To save his life, the little fuck could not keep his trap shut. Ever. That said, it's a quirk of fate in Freddy being the first of us to really speak to Doc. It has taken me the whole slog down here just to shake the rat loose from my tail—but I'm getting ahead of myself again.

Freddy McGuirre joined our little scout troop roughly six months before Doc Emmott. A kid like Freddy would be considered fresh meat, a candy-ass who ought to stay out of people's way if he knew what was good for him. But to Freddy, those first seven or eight months in the slammer probably felt like what the rest of his life had already been. A hyperactive foster child, he'd been in and out of JD schools most of his early life. When Freddy raped his twelve-year-old foster sister on his seventeenth birthday, the judge was only too happy to throw the book at him. I don't think I need to describe how much we disliked him.

Freddy came over to the table, dragging his feet with a plate piled high with beans and a couple of dogs sitting on top, their buns soaking up overcooked bean paste. He plopped himself down on the other side of Emmott, his gangly, freckled arms surrounding the tray like a fortress. I glanced over at him. I saw Floyd shaking his head, slowly, behind Dostoevsky.

"Hey, man," John Longman said, looking right at Freddy's stupid face, "those beans better not reveal themselves on the block later, when I'm tired and my patience for your bodily functions is low." Freddy stared at him. He didn't get it. He reached down with an unwashed paw and picked up a dog.

About two minutes of silence was all Freddy could take. With his mouth full as a river basin after the rainy season, he turned to Emmott. "Hey! Ain't you the guy 'at killed that society chick? A doctor, ain't you? How'd you do it, anyways? No gun, no knife, nothin'. Wow!" Freddy was overexcited. He was smiling hot dog.

Doc lifted his eyes and looked straight at him. I can hardly describe the expression on his face, but it made Freddy stop chewing, his copper-colored eyebrows touching his nose. His left eye moved, sort of, in what was not really a twitch, but more of an involuntary spasm. There was a long pause, and we did not hear shit out of him for the rest of lunch. I think I began to like Doc Emmott right about then.

A couple of weeks later, Floyd and I were shooting baskets on the exercise field, two screws watching and having a cigarette on the sidelines. Emmott, John Longman, and two other guys—Amos Sheehan and Teddy Stuttgard—came out to join us. The sky was a magnificent dark gray-blue, and a new November chill filled the air. A storm was on the way, bringing with it the kind of cold wetness that permeates the cell walls and gives birth to pneumonia. But in the meantime, a game of shooting baskets felt like a good workout, a last grab at fun before the storm clouds pushed us back into our cement tombs.

We were playing three on three: me, Emmott, and Teddy on one side; John, Floyd, and Amos on the other. My team was a little outclassed, being that both Floyd and Amos were big guys. Teddy was hefty, though, and I figured Emmott would just play for distraction.

Distraction is the word, all right. Emmott so completely surprised Floyd and Amos with his light, quick steps and an incredibly swift ability to dart around the opposing players that they didn't even know where to look for him. Emmott's small frame had always appeared stiff and reserved, but when he moved on the court, he was quick and alert, his sharp mind immediately seeing his options and taking them before Floyd's teammates could discern where he was headed. He gave us enough passes and shots to pull ahead, so that by the time Floyd's team had caught up, it only took four more shots by Teddy and me to win the game.

"Fuck all!" shouted Amos. "Goddamnit!"

The two screws jumped up from the bench, clapping and whistling.

Floyd wiped his brow and smiled a wide and happy smile. Amos was a sore loser, and it sure felt good to win over a sore loser. It was a great moment. One of those few moments in the twenty or so years I was at Cheyenne that put me only, and completely, in the present. And I don't have to tell you that is like a gift from the Almighty himself.

Teddy and I jumped up and down like pogo sticks and hollered, "Doc! Yeah, Doc! Way t' go, you *sonofabitch!* Too bad, Amos, you pussy!"

"Sore winners," said John with a shrug.

Just then, I felt a few singular drops of rain fall on my face. It felt great, that rain. Clean and cold. Wet cleansing my hot face, baptizing my senses. Finally, it started to pour. Floyd picked up the ball and trotted in. We followed back into the airless puce and brown gymnasium.

Just before we entered the building, Doc Emmott turned to me and said, "There's no place like home." There was a little humor in his voice then—not in his face, but the sound of it warmed me. He looked up at the sky with a deep breath, like a swimmer preparing for a dive.

I met up with John Longman later that evening in the rec room. He was sitting in a chair by the mesh-veiled windows carving a miniature figurine out of wood. He liked to do that; he made more than a hundred of the amazingly detailed things in the time I knew him. He got the tiny knife from a screw in exchange for ten bucks. Like I said, John was one of those rare inmates most everyone thought could be trusted, even with knife. He gathered pieces of branches that collected at the edge of the fence on the exercise field, hid them under his sweatshirt, then carved them expertly at night. He gave the pieces out on Christmas and birthdays. I myself got two diminutive ladies with long, braided hair and a tiny, stern-looking warrior.

I sat down on the windowsill and watched him. "Good game today," I said.

"Yeah. A good game."

"Nice detail on that leaf, man. Say, what do you think of Emmott?"

John paused for a moment, concentrating on scraping and shaping what was beginning to look like a little branch. Then he said, "Dr. Emmott's a man with fast feet, a fast mind, and a heavy conscience."

I considered, then nodded. I had trouble relating to John's reserved but deeply spiritual sensibility, but I admired his keen observations. Observation was our common ground.

As I've said before, I was glad to see John let out. Most of all, I was glad he left before the dogs came.

3.

I never really got to know Doc Emmott. I could say I never really knew anyone at Cheyenne. But if I did get to know

II

Emmott at all, it was around the end of 1979, two years after he arrived. John Longman was already gone, and the winter numbness was spreading through Cheyenne earlier than usual. I was in the library, thumbing through a photography book called *The Universal Picture*, one of my favorites, when I spotted Emmott sitting at a secluded table in a corner near the window. I took my book over and sat down with him. Neither of us said a word for a long time; I was preoccupied with photographs of an ancient Aztec ruin. *Mexico.* Blue-green water surrounding a land steeped in ancient history. It was easy to get lost in the idea.

I looked up. Emmott was reading the *American Pharmaceutical Journal.* I hadn't heard the page turn in a long while.

"Hey, Doc," I whispered, "what are you reading, man?"

He stared me straight in the eye. He said, "I put it in her coffee, Seamus."

For a second, I thought maybe he had finally cracked, disjointed conversation the first sign. Then I got it.

"Meperidine dissolves easily in hot liquid, even large amounts of it. It took effect when she got into the shower—she always took a shower after breakfast. There was a convulsion, more than I expected, but she was a small girl, Seamus. And, in the time we had been married, I never saw her eat more than half a grapefruit for breakfast. Her head hit the tub and cracked. It was a mess, as it turned out. I called the police before she even got into the shower."

I nodded, my eyes glued to his.

"I killed my wife, Seamus," he said again, his voice real quiet. I might have even heard it break. "I saw them together only once."

James Emmott was no sociopath, or whatever they call murderers these days. He was jealous, low-down, and guilty, just like every man on this planet who's lost his wife to someone else. He just went more than a little nuts over it.

The years went on the way they had been going. Some guys in for armed robbery left us, and so did Emmott's roommate, who had been in for repeated aggravated assault. They moved Emmott, and for a while, he had his own cell. Then he was paired with Don Harding.

Don was in for putting his sick, old mother out of her misery (though, we all imagined, he probably felt the misery was as much his). The worst thing anyone could really say about Don was that he had an unnatural attachment to a goldfish that he kept in a mayonnaise jar with holes popped in the lid. The fish was called Herb. No one thought it would last a day in that jar, but it did. Herb lived for five years on corn kernels and bread crumbs from the cafeteria. The day Herb died, Don missed breakfast, lunch, *and* supper. As Doc told it, Don dried Herb on their window sill, sealed him in an envelope, and slept with him under his pillow. No one saw Herb again, but it was thought that Don the Fish (as he became known) felt a little lump under his head every night for years to come.

Like I said, it was a good block for a while. Me, Floyd, Don the Fish, Doc Emmott, Amos, and Teddy had some good games on the court, even in the cold. The screws let us sweep the snow off the court with some old brooms, and we played 'til our hands were raw.

The winter of '82 was just like any other, complete with musty, damp walls and the shivers. We do all sorts of things here to help our time along. Cleaning the sties at a neighboring commercial pig farm if you're less than lucky;

making wood cabinets if you had any talent for it; doing laundry in the steaming-hot laundry room; fixing up government-owned vehicles and radios. I imagine the governor himself is riding around with one of my radios in his car, blasting "Proud Mary" or Beethoven's "Ode to Joy." But still, the time went slow.

Around late February, we started to notice a restlessness surfacing around some of the screws. Being locked up, we noticed things like that. Human emotion is the one thing inmates can observe freely. The guards or the warden, or both, were coming up with something, we felt. Something for us to do. Move us around, maybe. Rearrange us …

And then it happened.

One day, one of the screws brought a puppy in through the gates. My mate Floyd saw him do it. The guard was accompanied by Warden Parkes and a small, ruddy man in a navy suit. They got out of a black car with state government plates. The screw carried the pup in one of those tan kennel carriers, with a mesh window in the front and holes all around the sides. Floyd said he could see a wet, black nose quivering through one of the holes.

Rumors started flying around the pen and then eventually died down when no one heard or saw anything else. Until early spring when, this time, a bunch of guards brought five more pups through the gates.

About a week later, some cons were selected to "volunteer" for work. All of us were from the old ball court—myself, Teddy, and Amos, who was still a sore loser during game time. I liked all of us working together just fine. The guys were quiet and stable. In fact, we pretty much all were. Quiet, strong, and relatively even-tempered, as inmates go. Six dogs, three men. I should say pups, because that's what they were.

And they were beautiful. Brown, tan, and black; a curious mix of Bloodhound and Doberman is what they seemed, and all the same, too. Everything about them was warm and velvety: a soft, round puppy body nuzzling up against me with its innocent vulnerability. Especially Two and Five. They had no names, just numbers, but if I said it enough to them—*Come 'ere, Two; Good girl, Five*—the sound became names to my ears. It made me almost forget why I was there. Not *that* I was there, exactly, but maybe just *why*, the shadowy past fading into the act of caring for something other than myself.

It took our little group a while to figure out what we were doing with the dogs. First, we were instructed to put them through basic obedience training. We walked them in a circle several times a day, taught them to sit, heel, stay, come. Then, when they had mastered that, Warden Parkes gave us each a scrap of cloth, soiled and, I imagined, each scented differently. We gave the cloth pieces to the dogs so they could get the scents. Their wet, black noses moved carefully and thoroughly over the soft material. That was the beginning of it.

My first thought—dangerously altruistic—was that we were contributing to a new police or FBI squad, rescuing missing children or off-course hikers. I wanted to believe this. And yet I knew by the cool, detached tone in which Parkes spoke to us, the myriad of information purposefully withheld, that my idea was probably wishful thinking.

The first year, it all seemed like a good idea, at any rate. The dogs opened our whole world. The dark grays of the exercise yard, the cement walls, transformed into green and yellow grass tall as my knee and wind that cleaned my nostrils. Going back to those dark shadows and stale air of our cells seemed hideous in comparison. And they knew that, Warden Parkes and the screws. They knew how we had turned ourselves off to the outside world, how even Emmott, after a while, learned to fight off that deep, longing breath meant to soak up nature. And how, once exposed to it again, we would eventually need it like junkies need their dope.

I remember one night lying in the bunk, the blue light filtering down the aisle of the never entirely dark block.

"Floyd?" I whispered.

"Yeah."

"You awake, man?"

"Yeah."

"Those pups," I said, "do you know what they're up to?"

"Who is *they*?" he said.

"The warden—Parkes. That guy in the suit that stops by every week."

There was a pause. Then, "I don't know exactly what they are up to, Gideon, but I have some thoughts." The way he spoke, so solemn and steady, I didn't want him to finish his thought out loud.

There was another pause. So long this time that I thought he might have dozed off. I fixed my eyes on the steady columns of shadows on the floor, the phantom cell bars elongating out to the bed. And then Floyd said, "They're trackers, ain't they, Gideon? The dogs are trackers."

"Yeah, that's right. Like when hikers go missing up Whitetail Peak."

"Mmhm."

I let the thought work over me. We were teaching them tracking, all right. We all knew it and, in theory, what was wrong with that? Even when a prisoner escapes, you use dogs to find them. It was common practice. For the state police, anyway.

By spring of '83, the dogs had grown full-sized, their black noses shining in the sun of an open field. That's where we were standing, with the sun beating down on us and the clean wind whipping through our jackets. We were in the middle of a field of about fifteen acres, an unused plot of old farmland adjacent to the parking lot that bordered a vast forest of pine and oak, a place none of us had been and maybe only glanced at through a barred window.

We stood in a line, me and Amos, with only two of the six dogs. Our shackles had been replaced by radio collars. Warden Parkes and Navy Blue were standing behind us. There was also some little creep with a steno pad and pencil, as if ready to take notes on an historic event.

Our dogs were each tied with a six-foot lead, which we in turn held. Parkes looked at his watch. Teddy Stuttgard was suddenly called out of the kennels to join us on the field, which was just the first odd bit. Then he was given a head start of ten minutes, and now he lay somewhere at the edge of that forest (a radio collar clasped to his ankle in case he got any ideas). When the big hand hit the twelve, Navy Blue shouted an exuberant "*Go!*"

It took us exactly two minutes and thirty-eight seconds to find Teddy lying face-down in the thicket at the southwest corner where the field met the tree line. The dogs pulled on their leads and barked incessantly at Teddy until they were given the command to *stop*. *Sit*. They panted hard, and we breathed hard.

Teddy got up and brushed himself off. There was a pause filled only with the sound of winded breathing and the clumsy sound of dress shoes and suit trousers running through grass, closing in on us from behind. I heard Navy Blue shout, "Yahooooo!" He and the warden shook hands. The secretary got a conciliatory slap on the back.

After the first test, we didn't run another one for over a year. We sent the females off to mate and produce offspring. By the summer of '84, we had eighteen dogs, twelve of them puppies. It was becoming one big, happy family.

That winter, our own crew also grew. That snot-nosed, freckly little fuck Freddy McGuirre was added, and a guy named Bill Walker—also a strong, coordinated athlete. The round-out was the unexpected twist: Clark Howard *and* Doc Emmott. Seemed like they had really figured out just who was in our little clan (or very much outside it), though Floyd had somehow blessedly avoided the volunteer committee. It also seemed like the man-to-dog ratio was getting very uneven, if you asked me. Another thing: Doc Emmott, Bill Walker, and Clark Howard were forbidden to train or feed any dog but could only groom them and clean their kennels.

As for me, I always tried to hang around during grooming time. Emmott said I kept the dogs calm for him when he clipped their nails. Any chance I had to be with the dogs, I took. Two and Five remained my favorites, and I always felt like their offspring, Ten and Fourteen, knew how their mothers felt. Most of the dogs, in fact, knew me as master and pack-mate both, and they felt to me like some kind of family I never had.

I'll shorten the story here by saying yes, we continued to train, breed, and test the dogs. Once, when they tried to track me, they found me fine but stood patiently, though restlessly, surrounding me like a circle of confused hyenas. I lay in the prickly grass, the cold, damp ground beneath my hip, looking up into their bewildered, expectant faces. After seeing Teddy's run that first year, the whole project seemed safe and sort of interesting, and I'll admit it's what made me feel okay about being a target. But having almost a dozen hounds panting around me, their eyes wild, with only a handful of men to hold them back, made me wonder just how far the runs were going to go.

In the fall of 1986, Navy Blue—still a nameless enigma to us—showed up again. He had not been around since the new litter had grown, but this time, he arrived with five other men, all dressed like him. A few of them slung their jackets over their shoulders, beads of sweat forming on their brows.

Parkes came down to the kennels with them. He followed Navy Blue to the side and listened to the ruddy-faced fuckhole. With an expression I never could figure out, Parkes rounded us all up and had us bring the dogs to the edge of the field. As one of the men walked closer to me, I thought I could smell bourbon beneath aftershave.

Clark, who, as I said, had been mainly on kennel duty, was picked to go this time. We gave the cocksucker a head start of ten minutes. We had lengthened the time to give the dogs a better challenge. I know what I thought that day standing in front of those bastards, with their ties loosened, chuckling to each other some inside joke I couldn't hear. The others probably thought it, too. We had become the kind of entertainment, I thought, only a Roman could love; and I guess you could say I sensed a tension among the dogs that told me it was more than hide-and-seek going down.

When the big hand hit the twelve, we ran into the fields. Suddenly, the warden shouted, "Let 'em go! Let 'em go!"

"But Warden—"

"Drop the leads, goddamn it!"

And we did it. Out of fear or conditioning, or maybe some longing in all of us to see what might happen to Howard, we unleashed them and let them go on their own—and holy shit, did they run! Their long hind legs swooped ahead of their ribcages, and their haunches bobbed with every swift leap.

We found Clark Howard face down and screaming in a patch of tall, sharp grass, the dogs piled on top of him. Now Howard, as I've said, was a big guy, and a friend to many, he was not. But seeing him under eighteen keyed-up hounds made my blood run cold. The spectators came upon us gasping for air in their button-down shirts and patent leather shoes, their hearts working overtime just enough to allow one of them to cough out, in a wide grin, "Look at that! They got the son-of-a-nigger! Look at *that!*"

Howard came out of it all right, maybe because he had always been confident and dominant when he groomed them, or maybe just because of his imposing size; it was hard to tell. He had some bruises, a bite on the thigh, and a few deeper cuts from claws and tripping over sharp rocks. The following day, he limped into Parkes's office to beg for his old job back at the laundry. As I heard it, Parkes regretfully informed him that his former position was taken and that he would be wise to just forget about working at any other post.

We did not, after that, work another day in 1986.

One night, it was late April of this year, word got buzzing that our blue suits were about to pay us another visit. Seemed they had found the hunt a real thrill. We gathered together in the rec room—the ball club minus smart-ass Freddy, with Floyd sitting in for friendship's sake. We sat talking for hours, right up 'til curfew. Just shooting our mouths off and having a good time. Seldom were the evenings as benevolent and contented as that one was. It was the last time I saw the guys I had come to call my friends. And the last any of us saw Doc Emmott.

The very next day, he was picked. He stood at the top of the field, those green eyes hidden behind the reflection of his wire-rimmed glasses, his dry sense of humor clouded by rising panic. The leather lead dug into my palm as I barely held back a dog, and it burned as it slipped shamefully from my hand.

4.

So here I sit, in Puerto Angel, a little seaside village just south of Acapulco and to the north of *The Universal Picture's* Aztec ruins, sweating clean and breathing the moist, fresh air. How did I manage it? I don't honestly know. It's the question of the century, folks. Of course, I know how I managed it physically, but that's no secret. The dogs were not the only hazard on the job. The air was becoming increasingly dangerous for all of us. I could taste freedom in the stiff, itchy wheat and the soft, slick fur of the dogs; I could see freedom in their rippling muscles, tearing through the land as if it was only theirs.

So it didn't really surprise me much when I started getting that old point of view back: the awareness of the outside, the feelings of deprivation, all the ancient yearning that had been locked up twenty-one years in the cold cement tomb. And I am not a dim-witted man. Maybe not very cultured or worldly, and certainly not very motivated, but I know a chance when I see one. And with only four years to go before my parole hearing, I took it anyway.

I was partially betting on old Warden Parkes's conscience, which, from the look I saw on his face those last runs, I imagined was beginning to eat away at him the way a 'coon goes at week-old garbage. He could have caught us. I could almost see him looking through my back as I tore a sharp left through the edge of the forest, Freddy trailing me like an orphaned pup, leaving the bloody scene to fend for itself. As I bolted through the dense line of trees, I found myself panting, *"Quick as lightning, quick as lightning!"* willing Emmott's speed on myself. I only glanced back for one second—enough to know that not even Emmott was fast enough to escape the dogs.

There is a hot breeze coming into my bungalow right now, and that means it's time to head down to the water's edge. I couldn't stay inside at night for the first week or so. I often still sleep on the beach. I dream a lot about the fallow field and the damp shadows of the woods, and when I wake up screaming, I want to see palm trees and the moon sparkling on the endless ocean. I'll say one thing: seeing Emmott torn apart like that could have made any man stop dead in his tracks. But I ran. I ran faster than those hounds gaining speed and strength over their dog boy. Seeing Navy Blue and his bastards running toward their catch—well, that was justice enough for me.

Emmott, my friend, I wish I could send you one of those souvenir picture postcards: Breathtaking View of the Golfo de Tehuantepec. Got a sunburn that feels hot at night. Even lost Freddy. Just me and the ocean breeze. Time served well.

~ 1940 ~
Counting Sheep

Just before my seventh birthday, I got my lamb! Mrs. Overton said it was mine to keep and I could call it what I wanted, so I named it Sophie after Mama's sister who's still in Hannover.

There were three other lambs at the farm when mine was born, and three mamas and one papa. It was important that I counted them and made sure they were all together in the pasture before they got put back in the pen by the Big House where Mrs. Overton lived—I've known that ever since I was only five.

My lamb was called Little Snowy before I changed it to Sophie because the babies get their mama's names first of all. My mama was called Dr. Vonlinden by her patients and grown-ups like Mrs. Overton and her son Tom. Both them and Silas, who worked on the farm, called me Annie instead of Anja because they said it sounds more American. This was a good thing, they said. Especially since Mama had to work and people acted strange about her accent.

The farm wasn't for wool, but one day, Mrs. Overton said she was getting sick of potatoes and corn (even if she still grew them) and anyways, people always needed wool "with the war coming" (she was sure it was) and making it harder-than-stone for people to get the stuff they needed, never mind the stuff they liked. There was a man named Henry over in Amagansett who came and sheared the sheep. He bought the raw wool to make into yarn. Silas said he liked the sheep because they ate the fields we didn't use and he didn't have to mow as much.

I liked it best when Sophie and the others got to spend the week in the pasture next to our cottage. I could hear their bells at night clanging softly against their necks as they settled.

At night, after the sheep plunked down in the grass, I called to Mama and watched her tall, smooth walk, which made her look like Carole Lombard in the movies. She kneeled beside my cot and put her hand on the wool blanket. I liked to ask Mama questions at night, and back when we first came here, she always answered them. I was only four when we came, but I had lots of questions in me. I felt alone in our new world—I still feel alone even now, though I am almost eight—and the other place, the other life Mama and I lived, sometimes floated over both of us like a waiting ghost.

"At Oma Gertrude's farm, how many chickens were there? *Aben sie die Eier?*"

"In English, Anja."

"How many cats were there? What did Sophie wear to the dance with Heinerich? How did we get here? Tell me the story about when we left home."

I know we came from Germany, but I don't remember the trip. Well, I remember certain things: the fog coming over the boat; Mama holding my hand as we bumped together along the crowded sidewalk; the thick, scratchy hem of someone's coat hitting my cheek; the train rocking back and forth.

"I brought you with me, across the North Sea," said Mama. "We boarded a ship at Hamburg, where the wind was fierce. I had one suitcase, my black medical bag, and you. There was a conference in New York City at the Hotel Commodore. That is how I obtained the traveling papers."

The night before we left, everyone sat together at the large, shiny dining table in Opa's house—my mama, who they all called Karin, my Uncle Johannes, my Aunt Sophie, Oma Gertrude, and Opa Rudolf. Mama said I was sleeping on the sofa with a blanket Oma made for me. Opa Rudolf sat very still as Mama told them she was taking us to America. She said it in a quiet voice: "We have to leave now, before it's too late."

But Johannes stood up and began to shout. "Please, Karin! You can't just leave on your own, with a little one. Think of the danger."

"Early the next morning," Mama told me, "before dawn rose over the rutty cabbage fields, Johannes drove us to Hamburg. His little black car sped through the dark villages like a beetle through a garden. We passed over bridges where soldiers waited with electric torches to search his car. 'My wife and child,' he said as I held you close. 'Her sister is very ill—we just got word.' Johannes felt it necessary to say this, even though I had legitimate papers. It made us seem insular, an innocent family concerned only with getting to the next town." She stopped, thinking I went to sleep.

"Keep going, Mama." I closed my eyes because then I could see it in my head: the three of us driving on the dark streets.

"Your uncle was a good man," Mama continued, "and he understood my determination. He didn't want us to go, but," she said with a proud smile, "if we were going, he would be the one to take us."

"And Sophie?" I always asked about Sophie. In the picture Mama kept of her, she had a young and beautiful face, with bobbed blond curls.

"Sophie was the youngest. She was very pretty."

"But not as smart as you, because you are a doctor," I added quickly.

"*Sie müssen nicht das sagen*, Anja."

"She was happy with Heinerich because they were going to get married soon," I said. "He went to be in the army before we left. And you said to speak in English."

"Go to sleep now, Anja."

"The sheep are asleep, Mama. Listen, the bells have stopped."

The three lambs are sheep now, and there are also two new babies, the three mamas, and one papa. That makes nine. They are all in the pasture. It's important I see them all in there. Especially if something happens—a fox or a neighbor's bad dog, or a merciless thing like the Great Fire, or a storm like the Hurricane that came on so quickly last month.

There is a fox that lived in the woods behind the Big House. One morning, when me and Mrs. Overton were up by the barn checking corn ears, the sun already hot on our backs, we watched him walk right past us. In plain day! That fox turned his head and looked straight at me. He was like a red-haired dog with short legs and a too-bushy tail. His eyes were set deep inside his face: small, but human in a wicked way.

That was a while ago, before the Hurricane, even, but sometimes I dream about the fox. Well, not dream, exactly. I guess I don't dream too much lately, which is kind of strange.

In my imagination, I see the fox sitting at the kitchen table while me and Mama eat our dinner. He is glaring at us and scratching the edge of the table with his claws. Sometimes I think I see him looking into my window at night, putting his head down every couple of minutes to tear a piece of flesh from one of the sheep.

Our cottage has only one room with a stove and icebox and a table and my cot under a loft with a bed up a ladder where feed was kept long ago. That's where Mama sleeps. No one had lived in the cottage since Silas and his wife moved to a house in Eastville in Sag Harbor, where a lot of colored folks live. Town is fun to go to but is a little downtrodden. It used to be a rich whaling town, and now there are no more whales.

We moved to Mrs. Overton's farm two days after our boat came to Manhattan. We walked to Pennsylvania Station to get on a train. An old friend of Opa Rudolf told my mama stories about the island where Irish, Germans, and Italian peoples settled with the *Briten,* traveling out to the fresh air and country that reminded them of their old homes, out past the city where so many crammed together like bees in a hive.

Mrs. Overton had the farm with her husband when she was only nineteen. Her papa died and left it to her. Her husband was also dead when me and Mama came. She watched me when Mama was out on her rounds.

Mrs. Overton is very big. She's happy even when she's mad, which is a puzzle. She sure talks a lot. "Let's find something for those little hands of yours to do, Annie," she said when I was about four. "You like the horses? The chickens? You can't just follow me around all day, you know." No one rode the two old work horses, and Silas didn't make them pull the tractor now that they had a gasoline-powered one, but Mrs. Overton said she couldn't bring herself to sell them or put them down because her husband had loved them.

Most of all, Mrs. Overton talked about her family: her dead husband and her two daughters who married and moved away. Sometimes she talked about Tom, her son, and what a good young man he was living and working on the farm with her. She talked about when she was young while we checked white and yellow corn to send to the markets in New York.

"My husband Thomas was a catch in those days, and I was a dish myself, Annie," she said. "Thomas was handsome—tall with dark hair and green eyes, like Tom Junior. There were a lot of girls who were after him. After a month of courting, he said to me, 'You're pretty enough, and smart enough, to be my wife.'"

I nodded, wiping the sweat from my forehead. The skin on my hands, once soft with puckers, now were rough with blisters. Like small grown-up hands. "I'm thirsty, Mrs. Overton."

"You can go to the well when we're done. When we're *done*, Annie, you hear?"

I thought about Sophie and if she was okay in the field down by the cottage, and if she was thirsty, too. I couldn't see the sheep from up here at the barn, which I didn't like one bit.

"Did I ever tell you about my papa, Annie?"

"Yes, ma'am."

Mrs. Overton's papa was a blacksmith named Ben Halsey, and he died fighting the Great Fire that ate through Sag Harbor lots of years ago. It burned up Bay Street, wrecking Jared Wade's boatshop at one end, Ben Halsey's shop at the other end, and everything in between. The fire was stopped. "But not before taking the life of my father," said

Mrs. Overton. "He didn't survive," she liked to say, wrenching back a corn husk. "But the town survived."

The first time I heard that story, I couldn't stop thinking about it. There are so many dangerous things that could happen: fires, hurricanes, accidents. Like how I heard Silas and Tom talking about "the fiery glow" out on the ocean they could see at night and how no one was supposed to know about it.

For weeks after Mrs. Overton told me about her papa, I thought and thought about Ben Halsey's face, blackening and peeling as the flames burned his skin, his body falling away like cinders. I had no papa myself because he left Mama when I was a baby, but now I couldn't stop thinking about someone else's papa all burned up and dead. But then one day—about the same time I stopped dreaming—I just stopped thinking about it.

"You have to keep track of those sheep, Annie," Mrs. Overton said. "Though if the fox got in, you'd know it. You'd know it," she said, nodding.

I was told I had to count. Except I don't count, really, because I can tell who's there and who's not just by looking. I know them all. Especially Sophie, by her bright white belly, the rest of her plain and gray. Mama Junebug was fat with one ear that flopped a little, and Mama Snowy looked like Sophie but bigger. The papa was the biggest—a ram—and there was no thinking he was anyone but him. That can happen, I know, with people. Someone might look like one thing on the outside, but on the inside they might be something else. Just as me and Mama looked to the soldiers at the checkpoint in Hamburg. And then there was Heinrich, with his neat brown uniform and serious, almost empty expression. Only, he was married to sweet, pretty Sophie, so how bad could he be?

And then there is the way people look at me now, too. Or don't look at me. As if they are looking past me. Is it because they know I'm German? Or because of "what happened"? (Mrs. Overton said this more than once to Mama, though I have no idea what it means.)

At night now, Mama comes back from her house calls and rounds at the clinic. She sits quietly looking over at me or just past me out the window where the sound of the lambs' bells travel in. At night, I am sometimes overcome by a fearful urge to run up the ladder and climb into bed with Mama, hiding my head under the covers and wrapping my arms around her soft middle. I sometimes call up to her and, when I was little, she always came down to be with me. But not anymore.

When I was little, Mama made us warm milk, even in summer. Cold drinks chill the stomach, Mama said, and that's why Americans always have tummy aches. We drank our milk and I asked my questions, and then she told stories of Hannover and the little villages nearby. She described how she helped babies get born, fixed broken legs, and did surgeries. She told me, laughing, about the young men with measles or flu, and how when they saw her in her white coat and pretty blond hair pinned up, they'd yell: "A woman! I will surely die now!" And then how they quickly changed their minds.

Standing in the field, where I click my tongue and call to the sheep, I sometimes think of myself like Mama the Doctor. I am the sheeps' Protector, which is like being a doctor or guardian angel. I heard Silas say he thought I was an angel. When I was little, he used to tip his hat, his dark face shining in the sun, and say, "Little Bo Peep, how are your sheep?" He doesn't do that anymore.

I think maybe the War has made everyone so quiet, so different. But, no, it started before the War, around the time of the Hurricane. It's hard remembering that. The pictures inside my head are strong but fast, just like the pictures of when Mama and I arrived.

"I brought you with me, across the North Sea."

There are memories that float around in my head: the strange way the fog creeped across the boat like see-through fingers; the smells of people crowded on the city sidewalks; the bump and clack of the train.

When I remember things, I try to concentrate on the details: the patch of white under Sophie's belly; the sometimes flop of Mama Junebug's ear. It's important to remember those kinds of things, I know that. Something could happen and I'd have to be ready. But also there are things I don't want to think about—like the picture in my head of Mrs. Overton's father in the Great Fire. And the way the fox looked at me when he walked boldly past the barn in daytime. Or the way my mama's face looks now when she sits next to the radio at night, her plain gaze looking my way but not really *at* me.

Here are some things I do like to think about: winter, for one, which is so much better than looking for worms in corns ears on a hot morning. Winter, when the trees sound like they're groaning in the wind. Snow never comes on all at once, either, but in hours. It builds slow and grows thick, but I can mostly tell what's going to happen with it.

Well, summer is good on Friday afternoons when Mama takes me into town. We swim in the cold bay at the beach by the docks. "Here we are!" Mama says, wrapping me in a towel and planting kisses on my wet cheeks, "nice and warm now." Mrs. Bunday has a food stand at the beach for sandwiches and sodas. Then we walk up the block to Glynn's Theatre to see the double feature. One time, we saw *A Day at the Races* and *The Adventures of Robin Hood*; another time, it was *Bringing up Baby* and *Mr. Wong, Detective*.

I also liked Saturdays, when we walked to the highway where we caught the bus to Southampton to buy the *Berliner Zeitung* from Mr. Schulze. He sold newspapers from every country. Irish and Italian people, even Polish people from Riverhead, came to Mr. Schulze's store. He always wrapped up a little wedge of cheese from the deli counter and gave it to me. "What a lovely coat, Anja," he'd say in German. "*Sie sehen sehr hübsch aus.*"

One Sunday, Mr. Schulze gave Mama her *Berliner Zeitung* and said, "Do you agree with Germany's altruism, Dr. Vonlinden?" Mama took the paper from him and gave him some coins. "I hear their concern for the poor, diseased people in Russia is immense," he added, handing Mr. O'Donnell his paper.

Mama made her eyebrows go up and looked at Mr. Schulze with a look that said nothing except that she was listening to him. Then she took my hand and squeezed it hard as we walked without talking to the bakery, the newspaper rolled tight under her arm. After that, we didn't go to get the paper anymore. I heard Mr. Schulze wasn't allowed to sell it. Or, maybe something else had happened? I am not sure.

I think of a picture I saw of a soldier lying on the ground with his eyes open but his face ... I know he was dead. It was in the newspaper. Except that isn't right, either. Maybe it was someone else dead I saw.

At night, Mama loves listening to the radio, sitting straight up in her chair, smoking a cigarette. I like listening to the singers and the Ellery Queen mysteries, but I don't understand all of what the newsmen say; and what they do say scares me sometimes. Just the other night, I asked, "Mama, why do you listen to the news so much?" But she didn't answer.

"Are you listening to what is happening at home?" I looked around our clean cottage. I felt afraid; she was not listening to me. I made a sweeping motion with my arm that was more like pretending than believing. "We *are* home, you see? Mama? We can bring Sophie here, can't we?"

She said nothing but nodded a little. She kept nodding as if I was still talking or she was listening to something in her head. I thought I heard her whisper, "I brought you with me …"

"Mama, when will I see Uncle Johannes? Where is Oma Gertrude? Does Heinerich wear a uniform and march in the streets?" I ask these things from my cot, in the dark of the room, where I do not get the answers anymore.

When I was seven—in September—the Hurricane came, breaking everything apart like the bombs on the newsreels at the movies. My mama went to Lizzie and Jacob Strong's house down the road to help their first baby get born, so I had to stay with Mrs. Overton.

At one o'clock, terrible, scary winds blew, and the whole of Long Island was suddenly in the way of the storm. I was in a pasture near the barn when Tom came running. "Let's get them in, Annie. I don't like the feel of this wind." He held my hand tight as he pulled me toward the Big House.

Mama came back just in time for all of us to get down in the cellar. The grown-ups were all talking at once: "Have you any news from Guyers Farm? Hope the old lady got in—oh, but they'll be torn out for sure ..." and then, "Get down now, hurry!" Wind, wind, howling and ripping. Black sky overhead. Over and over they come; my flash-picture memories of this are more clear than the ones of being on the boat. But broken, too, the pictures. A puzzle with missing pieces so I can't put them together right. There was the cellar, the musty smell, the walls of potatoes. We were like moles in a tunnel: Mrs. Overton, Tom, Silas, Mama, and me.

By three o'clock, we could hear the sound of trees falling on the ground above us, their roots pulled from the rain-flooded earth, trunks crashing down over the cellar ceiling. As the eye of the storm came, the sun appeared through the black sky, and I think I heard later that some people went out to see the broken trees and things only to get caught in the storm's returning.

"Don't do it, Mrs. Overton," Silas said, gently grabbing the big woman's arm as she went for the stairs. "It's only the eye." I remembered the fox's eye: red and gleaming. Did all the sheep get into the barn? Did I remember to get them all in? Someone was grabbing my arm, now, too. There was a loud crash above my head on the cellar doors. Then water, water. *Water.* I heard a scream—Mrs. Overton? Mama? Snowy? Can the ewes scream for their babies if they are scared enough?

The Hurricane ended. A neighbor got the tree up from the door with his tractor. I don't remember this, but I know it.

Everywhere was damage. The old, big trees that were on Main Street were gone, ripped up and smashed like a giant had stepped on them. Mrs. Overton started selling axes, saws, and kerosene lamps. She always knows what people will buy. Mama was called to fix the hurt which, for some reason, no one wanted to let her do. And the people who died in the storm needed to be identified, and also two ladies had babies the next week after.

Meantime, I lay on my cot. Alone in the cottage. It felt like I was left for hours or days, it was hard to tell. Then, in my memory's eye, it was late fall and I was in the pasture again with my sheep.

Houses have been built and windows fixed; almost everything was repaired except the steeple of Old Whaler's church that is still not put back. I hear a lot of people saying that time beforehand will be known as "before the Great Hurricane," the same as Mrs. Overton's mother called history "before the Great Fire." Things are different for me and my mama, too. Mama has more patients and more rounds at the clinic now. She doesn't tell me stories like she used to.

But there is also the War. And, though we ran ahead of it in the dark of night with a good head start, it seems meant to catch up with us anyway.

Anything could happen. That's the thing. Like the Hurricane, or the Great Fire. Or the War. Or the red glow over the ocean at night that people aren't supposed to talk about. Things can come on suddenly, with no warning or with a warning that no one paid attention to. It's important to look up at the sky every moment or so, not just close my eyes against the warm sun, but to make sure there aren't clouds swooping in from the Nor'east, dark and fast-moving. If that happens, I have to round up the sheep right away.

Since the fox killed Little Bessy last week, Mrs. Overton got a dog. His name is Laddie, and he is pretty good at guarding the sheep in the pen at night over by the Big House, but he isn't very good at rounding them up to move them. He hangs around me mostly, sometimes looking at me with sad eyes that have dark markings like the coal-lined eyes of a Hollywood movie star. I think he must be the only one who still looks at me as if I am really next to him. I want to give him a new name, like Flynn, but I better wait 'til Mrs. Overton is in a good mood, one of her talky-cheery moods. In the meantime, I just kind of wander around, trying not to think about the tufts of fur and spots of blood that were all that was left of Little Bessy. I want Sophie to sleep *inside* the cottage now on the rug next to my cot, but I can't find a way of asking.

It's middle of July, the air cool but not moving. It seems like yesterday it was spring, and the day before that it was fall. Night has happened quickly again, and I don't remember how it turned from day to sunset. A heat wave is coming. I can feel it.

I lie down half-sleeping, half-thinking of Sophie in her pen when there comes a knock at the door. I see Mama in her nightgown and robe come down the ladder and go to the door, her face looking watchful.

"What is it, Mama?"

"Who is it?" Mama whispers to someone else. She unlatches the door.

I hear the sound of a man's voice, then another, both polite.

"Come in," Mama says. One man says something that I can't hear. "No," says Mama, her voice harsh and wavering. "That's my daughter's. You can take the floor by the stove."

"Thank you, ma'am," says the one man, the first one I heard. "We greatly appreciate this. It's been a long journey."

"What journey? He exaggerates, Doctor," says the other. "He's got land-legs from fishing too long. Fishing, you see? Never mind—my hand is fine—it's just a nick from the hook. There's some bass for you on the step outside. We didn't want to stink up your lovely house."

"Thank you." Mama's voice remains hushed, I think, so it won't wake me, even though I am already awake. She helps the men settle, gets a plaster for the one with the cut on his hand, then goes back upstairs.

My body is tired and I want to drift off again. I see the forms of the two men taking their slickers off and lying down in front of the wood stove. I'm not afraid of them because I can sense that Mama must know them. Mama sometimes helps people at funny times. More than once, someone came to the door in the middle of the night, and only in the morning did I hear it was Jacob Strong come for some cough syrup for the new baby, or Mrs. Bunday, the sandwich lady from the beach, sending her husband down for medicine for one of her bad headaches.

The men lie down, pushing on their jackets like pillows. One of them looks over where I am. "A perfectly good bed going to waste." His voice sounds almost spiteful.

"Never mind," says the other man. "We're not staying long."

I smile at the stranger. I think about what I can do to help them. Would Mama mind if I put the kettle on and made them some tea?

When the sun rises, the two men are gone, and my mama is packing some bottles and needles into her bag. She says nothing about the visitors but rushes out in silence.

The heat is standing still now, not getting hotter but not getting cooler either, even at night. There is no wind. The ocean and the bay are flat like lakes. I really want to give the sheep water from the well, but once, in another summertime, Mrs. Overton caught me at this. "Stop wasting water on those damn sheep! If this drought keeps up, there won't be any for us, let alone the corn." This seemed funny, because not only was Mrs. Overton sick of corn, but just six miles south and three miles north was all the water anyone could hope for. "It's *salt* water," Mrs. Overton had snapped, shaking her head.

Henry, the man from Amagansett, came and sheared the sheep the other day, but I know they are still hot because they sit around not moving, like statues. When no one notices, I try to get Sophie into the shade of an old maple tree—kiss, kiss, kiss—holding my hand out like a treat is in it. About an hour later, Tom comes down to the pasture next to the cottage and leaves a bucket with water in it. He doesn't look in my direction. I am still sitting under the tree waiting for Sophie. Tom doesn't say much ever, but he is a good man. He must be to bring Sophie water when his mother doesn't want the sheep to have any. It isn't easy to tell if people are good or not, even if I am sure they are because my mama was nice to them or helped them out.

Like the men who came and stayed the night two weeks ago. I really haven't thought of them since; I don't wonder or think about their faces when I lie awake in my cot at night. It was hard to see their faces anyway, it was so dark. I don't know if I am making them up in my head to be young or old, with beards or red or brown hair.

And now it is so hot, the cool of that night gone quickly in a strange dream. I lie down next to my lamb, who is all grown up—did she really grow up that quick?—and put my head on the grass. The dog, Laddie, stretches out close by, his fur sticky and thick from jumping through the stream in the woods. I think I fall asleep, because when I open my eyes next, the sun is lower on the sky—still hot, but more orange than white now—and I know Mama is coming home soon. I go up to the north pasture, where I figure I should feed the horses. Back at the cottage, I find that my mama is not home and ... how did I get back here so sudden?

I walk back up the path to the Big House, moving slowly in the heat. It's just too hard to run; I feel like I am walking underwater. I think of going swimming, of floating in the cool bay.

Then, without warning, I feel a rush of water down my throat that catches my breath and makes it stop.

I choke and wheeze. Horrible!

It is a feeling more than an imagining, as if it really is happening.

I steady myself—gasping and blinking into the hazy sunlight. I wipe my eyes, tears coming from them. Goodness, I am scared for a minute! Where is Mama, anyway? Oh, yes, up at the Big House.

The kitchen door is wide open, but the inside is made dark by the screen door, and I can see Mrs. Overton and Mama sitting by a window drinking lemonade. Mrs. Overton's round face leans toward my mama's. Then something makes me step back. I duck down and lean on the house under the window, peeking just over the sill to see them.

"They landed at the beach in Amagansett," Mama says.

"Oh?"

Mama looks steady at Mrs. Overton. "From a U-boat," she says. "I read in the paper that there were eight of them, four heading south to Florida, and four to scatter around the Northeast. But only two came to me. You understand me, yes?"

"That sounds far-fetched, Karin, don't you think? Have some more lemonade." Mrs. Overton's face is smiling, yet there is something in it that seems terrible and fake.

"*Mein Gott*, Marjorie, what do you think Jacob Strong and his brothers saw last week down at the beach? Fireworks? Silas and Tom go down at night to watch the explosions on the horizon and make certain they aren't getting closer. They are right off Long Island—the *Unterseeboot*—we all know it. Even if the newspapers are told not to say."

I realize what Mama has said. It's like in the newsreels before the movies, except it's here where we live, and how come no one told me?

"Well, it's done now; we don't need to speak of it."

"Then you believe me? You agree it could have been them?" My mother leans forward, stretching her fingers on the table with excitement. "They spoke perfect English; that's what the newspaper said." Mama lowers her voice to a whisper and adds, "No one would suspect they were not American."

Mrs. Overton sighs. "All right, then what happened?"

I shift on my hips. I can feel the sweat start to run down the sides of my face, but I don't dare move. What does Mama mean the men were not American?

Mama looks up at the ceiling, breathing deeply. "Two of them came to me. Someone must have told them I am

German. That I might help them." She looks very seriously at Mrs. Overton. "That man Schulze, from the deli?"

Mrs. Overton shakes her head, shrugging her shoulders. Then she smiles. "It's done now, anyway."

"They buried explosives in the sand on the beach, the newspapers say," Mama goes on. "They were dressed as fishermen. It was clever. But they were," she lets out a strange laugh that doesn't sound like anything funny, "they were not the brightest, these men."

Mrs. Overton shakes her head. "Explosives? I don't think so. No, not—"

"They were approached by a young coast guardsman. Just a teenager, but he was very suspicious."

"But the boy didn't stop them, did he? You see? He let them go. They *were* just fishermen."

"Marjorie, I do not think you understand."

"You said they spent the night with you?"

"Yes. The coast guard boy was afraid, so he played along with them, you know, discussing the catch and the weather, then he let them go. Then they must have gotten on the train, but got off again in Bridgehampton and stopped with me here, afraid they were being followed. The last I knew, they were on a train again to Manhattan. Back to their homes, they told me. They said they were fishermen come out from Manhattan."

Mrs. Overton is quiet again. I'm still trying to understand about the explosions. Where will they happen? Here?

"They were caught," Mama says. "They caught them yesterday. They will be executed."

Mrs. Overton nods, her eyes looking down.

"And you knew nothing about this?"

"About what?" Mrs. Overton says, the brightness coming back into her voice in a way that makes me even more uneasy. Then she speaks quietly. "It is good of you to help people, Karin. One shouldn't forget one's countrymen. Even in war. My mother, rest her, was a Brünnerman. All this talk of war with Germany. We're a good people, Karin."

My mama covers her face with her hands. "You don't know what you are saying. If only you knew." She is silent for a bit. Then she says through her hands, "I left it all behind. For Anja's sake."

"Well, let's not think about *that*. It couldn't be helped. We all tried."

Now I am trying even harder to understand; were they talking about the fox? I should have tried harder. I should have watched Bessy all the time.

"They had plans for me," says Mama. "Experiments, research. Unspeakable. I could not raise her there." She looks up at Mrs. Overton, who now seems less jolly.

"Of course you did what you thought was best."

"I didn't know who they were! It's true what they say in the papers; no one would know these men are not American."

"Not that again, Karin, please."

"I thought they were fishermen, tired and cold from their day. One of them had a bad cut on his hand from a hook. How could I have known? And now they will come after me. And for what?"

My heart is jumping. Who will come after Mama? The men who spent the night? The police? I don't understand. Fear splashes over me like a huge wave.

"Shh. Have some more," Mrs. Overton says, filling Mama's glass so that it overflows on the table.

"I told them I was not interested in changing my position, but they persisted."

"Karin, please. I don't even know what you're talking about."

I watch my mama take a sip of lemonade and try to wipe up the spill with her handkerchief. The handkerchief has an embroidered *K* on it. Oma Gertrude made it. Now it is wet and discolored a pale yellow.

"I received phone calls first at my office," she says, though her face is like dreaming with her eyes open. "They told me there were projects for me. That the doctors of Germany would lead the world in medical achievements. I would have the opportunity to find cures for diseases that have eluded us for centuries. *Diabolisch!*" Mama makes a laughing-coughing sound that scares me. "When they began calling me at home, at night, I began to worry about Albert."

"Albert? Who is Albert?" says Mrs. Overton, coming alive again.

I wipe my forehead. I've never heard of Albert before. Maybe he is a brother of Heinrich's. No, he has three sisters. I once got Mama to tell me that. Three sisters, and they all loved Sophie. Pretty Sophie, she was so easy to love.

"Dr. Albert Rubenstein," says Mama. "He was my assistant. Of course, he was under me in rank at the hospital, but really, he was the best surgeon I have ever known. And kind. Unlike Martin."

I never heard my mama talk of my papa like that. She really never talked about him at all. And now there is Dr. Albert, her friend who was nice and good. I want to come away from the window, go back up the path to find Sophie, and lie back down with her in the shade. Maybe I can pretend I never walked up to the Big House in the first place. I will lie down and sleep in the shade with Sophie until Mama comes home. But my feet are rocks.

"I should have known. But I was still hoping and telling myself this was not happening to my country. Many people did not care about what happened to the Jews."

Mrs. Overton smirks at this.

"But there were some of us who saw that our country was only headed for self-destruction. And worse than that."

Mrs. Overton's mouth turns down; her eyes roll up as she shrugs.

"I kept asking myself, what could I do? Until it was too late to think of anything. Albert and I were in the laboratory, noting the results of a test for a new patient. Headaches, I remember the woman had headaches, and Albert wanted to rule out any blood disorders or tumors. Frau Klose, the nurse on duty, came running into the lab. There were soldiers at the door demanding to see me, she said. But then she looked at Albert with an expression that said, 'It's you they want.' Before she could say anything more, they had come into the main hall, just outside the lab."

In my mind, I see soldiers, like the ones in the newsreels before the double feature. In my mind, there is a crash of doors being slammed open, boots banging on the tile floor.

"Albert shoved the patient's files into my arms," Mama continues, her thin, shaky hands acting out what happened. "'Put these away,' he said. He was afraid that all the work we'd done to help this woman would be wasted. They came in. There was no time to hide him, no place for him to go. Part of me believed I could handle the matter later and everything would be fine, that he would be released.

"They grabbed Albert by his arms so roughly that his glasses fell off and shattered on the floor. I grabbed hold of his other arm. We, each of us, pulled, but he slipped from me. One of the soldiers touched my cheek as if something romantic had just occurred. *Widerliches Schwein.*"

I can see her hand wipe the tears off her face. She sucks in a breath slowly. "I never saw him again."

Mrs. Overton is not talking. She doesn't move, doesn't try to pour Mama more lemonade or touch her hand the way I want to. But I can't move, either. If I move, they will hear me, my feet rustling against the dry grass that grows next to the house.

I better move sometime, though, because I'm supposed to go back to the cottage and pretend I was never here. I slide my foot away from the house, and for the first time, I realize that, actually, I do not make a sound at all. There is no scrape or crunch on the dry grass. My foot moves silent like the dead. I listen out into the air. I can hear the faraway sound of a sheep's bell. Silas's hammer on a fence post. A seagull calling. It is only me who doesn't make a noise.

I see the broken glasses of Mama's assistant, the frightened man dragged off by soldiers, the sound of crashing doors, and this time I know his terror, too. I feel the soldier's grip on my own arm, only it is really Silas grabbing me with both his big hands and almost tearing my arm off my body.

I hear him yell, "Bo Peep, get back here! It's only the eye!" and hear another crash of a tree above—but I saw sunlight, didn't I, coming through the crack in the cellar doors? I hear my mama scream. Shrill as a crow. Then loud and moaning, like the sound of a ewe with its throat torn open. Then there's pain like I've never felt. My head pounds; my lungs feel like they are bursting inside me. I can't breathe!

Sharp pain is coming into my whole body—oh, help!—as I try to put air in my lungs. In front of me, I see the strange angle of the cellar door ripped open, but upside-down, and a huge tree branch reaching sharply in for us. Silas's face peering into mine, and the sound of my mama wailing. Then everything in front of me is going gray—a pale, ugly gray that hurts to look at. I try to speak but can't. I want to say *Mama, Mama, Mama,* over and over again and maybe I am, but everything is going away so quickly and the gray light is worse, and the water is rushing down on me now, and the taste of salt—of blood—filling my mouth until I stop feeling anything at all.

Mama and Mrs. Overton sit in silence in the Big House kitchen. Then, Mrs. Overton pushes her chair behind, stands up, and says, "Well. I think I'll call Tom in for supper."

I have to listen carefully at night for the sound of their bells. Without a full moon, I can hardly find their round, low shapes in the pasture outside my window. I try to lead Sophie to a bed of hay just under the window next to my cot and tell her to stay put, don't get up 'til morning, but of course I know now that Sophie can't hear me. No one can.

I think about the fox but, truthfully, it's not his face that I see in my mind's imagining. It is the face of a man—long and afraid—his glasses falling from his face, his eyes blind and white, his skeleton hands feeling along the tile floor for broken glass. The face looks more like I imagine Ben Halsey and sometimes it, too, catches on fire and falls away. I don't know what Albert the doctor's face really looked like. I never saw a picture of him or heard him described. And I do not see him here, where I wait among the living, though I am beginning to wonder if this is where I am supposed to stay forever.

On my cot, in the dark, I think about calling up to my mama. There is such a silence here all the time now, my mama looking close-lipped in my direction from across the table, her eyes glassy and not reaching mine at all. She listens to the radio for a bit, then goes to bed early. I try to reach out and grab her skirt, pull myself to her and cry. But it doesn't work. I want so bad to feel her, but she can't feel me no matter what.

My legs stretch outside the sheets, and I lie still against the heat in the dark, airless cottage. I listen for Sophie's bell. I'll go out there if I need to, if I hear them move away from their spot under the maple tree. Laddie is no good at guarding, I am sure of that; I can practically hear him snoring from in here. The fox could sneak into the pasture so easy, right under that dog's nose.

I think about calling up to Mama, but I can't think of what to ask her. I close my eyes and there is a flash of cement sidewalk on the way to the train, the crowd of bodies moving together, the rocking of the train as it goes fast away from the city and closer to here. And my mama's voice, whispering, "We came from Hannover. I brought you with me across the North Sea."

~ 1971 ~
Forever Jim

I was born in Beauvais in 1906. My father made buttons for the bright yellow coats that *les pompier* wore. When they rode down the rue St. Germain or rue Jean D'Arc in their motorized truck, alarm bell ringing madly, I waved to them. If my brother was with me, I would bend down and say, "Wave to the men, Claude; they are wearing Papa's buttons into the fire."

My mother had roses in her garden; I remember this. They were beautiful—red, yellow, and apricot, and big as my hand. They grew up the side of our gray stone house, clinging to a white-painted wooden trellis that Papa built for her when I was still very small. The trellis stayed there, leaning against the south side of the house for years. The paint chipped away to reveal wood the color of mortar, the roses stretching wildly, un-pruned, into the air. Maman's roses also grew on straight stalks in the backyard. Many of the pink ones were higher than Claude, who never lived to outgrow them.

I came here in 1968. Years ago, if I had been told I would settle in such a place as this, I would not have believed it. Then again, I might not have believed other things as well—things that seem aberrant when thought of or spoken about, things that women may fear but never really believe will happen to them.

But here I am, in the Cimètiere du Père Lachaise, and it is much better than where I could be. Before this, I stayed alongside La Madeleine Opéra, on the side near the Boulevard Malesherbes, where an unused doorway served me well on windy days. At night, the train station Gare St. Lazare proved a safe and comfortable place. Then, one day, my friend Madame Frontier (who was as unfortunate as I) said to me, "Nanette, I know a better place for you." Her voice was a whisper that echoed in the tunnels and vanished with the sound of the Metro—swooshhhh—on its way to the Republique or St. Sebastien Froisard.

I know a better place, she said.

The trees are making a sound like that. *Sshhhh.* Right now, as the cold wind moves slowly through their two hundred years. I can see their tops and a thousand of their drying leaves in the moonlight. The sky is nearly black, the moon white as an opal. I can see all this but not much else from Monsieur Armand's chamber. His home is mine tonight: the shadowed walls speckled with moss, the floor soft with fallen leaves blown in with generations of infrequent family visits. Armand rests in stone next to me, but I have my soft bed of leaves.

Ah, and here is Michelle. Her orange and white fur and warm, fat body pressing against my shoulder. She rumbles with comfort in her throat. Her tail swishes gently, tickling my arm. On my other side is Georges, his paw tapping my cheek. *Make room, make room for Georges!* His gray warmth finally settles against my back. His green eyes glow red and deceptively sinister in the dark when he looks at me. He and Michelle will keep me warm, which is a gift for stiff bones at my age.

Tomorrow, we'll move so I can be closer to Chopin. Every now and then, I leave him alone. Leave him to the trees and yellow flowers planted at his angel's feet. But I'm always back again before too long. Sometimes I go to Madame Piaf, but Lulu has trouble finding me there, up the steep hill, with her limp and sore pad. So tonight, it is Armand, as it has been for three nights now. That's fine with me, and it's fine with them.

When I first arrived here, there was a dusting of snow on the ground. Also, there was a curious lack of color. I am ashamed to say I was afraid. I had heard stories that below the hallowed ground lay untold graves from the Revolution, too many victims to bury properly; later on, they were merely covered over with new vaults instead. I thought of old superstitions and ghostly tales Grandmere used to tell me (don't light a cigarette with a candlestick; never place bread on the table upside down). I remembered the dares my friends and I would concoct for each other in the churchyard at home in Beauvais, the setting sun like blood behind the spire. *Sit with your back resting on the headstone until dark, and tell us if a hand came up to grab you ...*

Then I saw the way the snow carpeted the winding, dull, gravel paths before me as I entered the back gate by the Boulevard Arago, the way it silenced the motorcars and clung like candied sugar to the immense charcoal branches of the trees.

And I felt young again, standing there, as I was when Paul first came to the flat on the Ile St-Louis where I lived with three other young women. Like the city, we were beautiful then. I had bobbed hair and a chartreuse green satin gown, and it was snowing. The icy flakes fell lightly and silently around us, glittering on my long, black eyelashes. Paul was a gentleman, dashing and strong; he gave me his arm as we walked. *Maman, if you could have seen him.* The snow fell so softly that night, without a breeze, like confetti dropped from an open window on New Year's Eve. The next morning, the sun rose pink against the still, white dusting of snow as Paul and I walked back to my flat, the wine still swimming in my head.

That's how it was the first day I arrived here: snowy and beautiful. I do not miss Paul as much now that I am here. Instead, I wait for the day I will see him. It was not his fault I was left alone. Well, I do not blame him at any rate. How could we have known the cancer would take him in less than two months? Or that Papa would squander his good savings in grief after Maman died? Perhaps Paul should not have relied on the assumption that my frail and failing Papa would have provided for his aging daughter. Maybe I should not have assumed that one of them would always protect me. I had only ever trusted Paul and Papa, at any rate, for I know how men can be.

Oh, I am standing at Chopin again, aren't I? My finger has been running along the edge of my lashes again.

Stop, says Paul, *you will thin them if you keep it up.* But I cannot seem to help it since the night I worked late at the office with M. Regal. It was at his insistence. I was a modern woman, after all, and who would have thought he did not view me as an equal? As someone to be respected and relied upon for her help managing his business. Didn't we work alongside each other for the sake of work alone? And here it comes now—the moment of everything changing—though I am trying to stop it. Paul was driven to wipe it out, to eradicate it from my memory and his. "The man should go to prison," Paul had hissed, urging me to go to the police. But it was bad enough what that doctor put me through two months later, and the doctor who, afterward, had to fix his blunder; how was I to face the police? Mon Dieu, *Paul, you've even agreed to marry me though I will never have children now. Even though there are still times when your touch makes me wince as though I am a young girl, the hand from the grave actually reaching me this time.*

 It's good to know Paul is somewhere with Chopin and Seurat. And the Madames Piaf and Bernhardt, as well. They were good women. Their hair was also bobbed.

It was because of the snow that they found me. I was never fond of cats, so I would not have approached them. Not that I disliked them. They were simply unfamiliar. We had two dogs when Claude and I were young, but I don't remember their names. These cats, I know. Chatouiller came first—his black nose wet and glistening on his noble *visage noir*. His body was immense, and he mastered the trees like a leopard from some distant jungle. He seemed to need no one. And yet on the coldest morning in February, with slick ice covering the pathways, I awoke to find him curled next to me, a spoon of thick, black fur and pale blue eyes.

 Chatouiller hangs back under the stones and lampposts when the others come around, but he is always near. He needs no one. Yet he needs me.

As for Georges and Michelle, they are a constant. And Lulu, with her limp, and Tigre and Badinage. As constant as Pierre who comes to clean the angels, cherubs, and phantoms whose stone cloaks—carved to look as if in motion—blow in the silent wind of the dead. Pierre is always in brown, a drab outfit from neck to ankle.

In the spring, Pierre says, "Nanette, you are still here."

"Yes. Where else would I be, tell me?"

Pierre smiles at me in his crumpled city uniform. He says something kind to Badinage, pats his tortoiseshell head with soil-streaked fingers. Badinage eats Madame Ducout's flowers. "Her husband complains," says Pierre, pointing to Madame's resting place. I shrug. Pierre gives me a can of salmon.

At night, I open it, and we all have some. It's good and salty.

Maman used to salt the fish Papa caught with Claude from the river. At the table, Claude could never keep still. We used to scold him, then laugh at his silly expressions as he ate. He was like a little spark, shining exuberance on our family. After he was gone, his place at the table seemed like a hole into the earth. Like the damp, root-torn hole in which we buried him. We didn't know why he went down to the bank by the Sonnier's farm, when he knew the proper fishing river so well. His small, bloated body was found in the overflowed stream instead, which made little sense, either, since it was more shallow than the river. *Maman, you were so lost. If you were here with me now, you would see the tiny markers, the little ones sleeping peacefully like Claude. If only he were here with me, instead of far away in the countryside.*

After Claude died, there was no more of Papa playing the piano, his beautiful renditions of Chopin, Debussy, Ravel.

The music had once filled our house like Claude's light and laughter. *Papa, please let me go, I can't stay here in this house any longer.*

In my memory, most often, they are as they were when I was a child. My father may have made buttons in the factory, but he wore a suit on Sundays, played the piano, tipped his hat to people when he took us into town. Maman wore gloves out, always. I wore a pair of her gloves the night Paul first came to take me out. I was modern; I bobbed my hair, wore deep red lipstick, and worked as a secretary for a businessman on the Right Bank. M. Regal, it was. I cannot seem to forget him. I've promised Paul not to think about that again, haven't I?

But my dress was made of chartreuse satin—have I said?—with indigo blue sequins I had sewn myself in the likeness of Maman's roses. I can think about that. My skin was powdered porcelain, my lashes long and black.

"The world is changing, Nanette," Pierre says to me one day. I have been here almost three years. This place, now my home, has been the same for almost two hundred years. Here are those who survived the Revolution, though none of their descendants come to visit them anymore. The world is always changing, and it is always the same. Here, especially, in this city-within-the-city, a tightly knit village of stone and flowers and ancient trees, it is never-changing. "I don't understand what you mean, Pierre," I reply. "Nothing changes here."

"You will see, Nanette," Pierre sighs.

"What will I see?" I look next to us at a crypt marked *Rosemonde 1832*. I look behind me. "What will I see, Pierre? Are they changing the paths? Cutting down the trees?"

"Shh, it's alright. Don't be afraid. In here, it's the same for now. I'm speaking of the world outside."

"Oh," I say, feeling myself breathe deeply. "That doesn't matter."

At night, we sleep, Lulu and I, up the hill past Mme. Bernhardt. The quiet creeps over us like a mist of peace, not even a lone tourist to trouble us.

But the next week, a young woman with long, red hair appears. She comes discreetly, with a man in a dark suit who is no friend of hers. She wears a long, quilted skirt and wool coat. Her cheeks are raw from crying, her eyes hollow and half-sleeping. Yes, I can see her. *Shh, be quiet, Badinage—Georges, do not provoke!—or she will look our way and notice us. Do you see how she stares, disbelieving, at the box Pierre and his sons carry?*

I watch from behind ancient Maurice, his likeness in stone shielding me from her grieving, distant eyes. She strikes me as something otherworldly, with her loose, tousled hair—how do they not plait it or upsweep it these days? And her expression. Sad, but a bit fearful as well. As if she does not want anyone to find her.

It is soon after this that they come. With their long hair, the men like Chopin himself, all in coat tails or vests. And the girls in long, flowing skirts, sheep's wool blankets draped around their shoulders. Many of them, the men and women alike, wear flowers in their unkempt hair, as Maman did with her silky curls when she was a girl, and even painted flowers on their unshaven faces—a daisy on the cheek, a heart next to the eye. They cry and leave pieces of paper, sticking them with chewing gum on any surface they can find. The notes saying, "Search on man, calm saviour, veteran of wars and calculable greed. Godspeed and forgive you. Morning star, fragrant meadowperson girl ..."

The poetry is fragmented, like disjointed Byron. Perhaps I should not be so disconcerted, but I find myself confused and frightened whenever I come upon a new verse. Here is another one. *Tigre, do you see how they have marred the outside of Madame Bordenave's wall?*

I go to visit M. Apollinaire—for who is a more famous poet than he? I pinch the dead blossoms from the flowers lining either side of his marker. *It is just like taking care of Maman's roses, Monsieur. Do not worry; your garden will be beautiful again.*

And what of me? Will Pierre or his son remember to leave me a blossom or two now and again? I would not mind if only Pierre is there to see me buried. He has promised me a place, even if it's a secret kept from the city planners. But I wonder now, as the faded red petals of Apollinaire's begonias stain my fingertips like blood, if there will be a space left for me. Each weekend brings new crowds, and I notice Pierre working harder to dig for each new interment in time. It seems the red-headed woman's husband has made this place something of a fashion, like sequins and fringe, coal-lined eyes and jazz, and all that is still so real to me.

Eventually, the young people's scrawled words leave marks etched or painted on other resting places as well, spreading out like a kind of *épidémique* past the lifeless bust of the man that has been erected in his honor. M. Maurice's cracked marble nose is gone before the year is out, chipped off by a small brass pipe and a careless laugh. By the next, the side of the Le Mans's wall is covered in painted words and American curses.

Every Saturday, the school children still come to see Chopin. But I hear them asking, "Where is the other one, the singer? I want to see him." Pierre tells me this man was a poet.

I say, "Did his words rise above the music of masters? Did they touch the heart of a thousand people?" Pierre does not think so. I do not. But I never knew him. The sounds of his piano, of his etude, did not fill my father's living room.

I walk through the back gate with my bag in my arms. Today is good. Lulu will have her ointment for her paw. The others will eat rice with some *boeuf haché* mixed in. I can feel the dampness coming back quickly now that the sun has gone down. But I have an extra blanket today from a rubbish bin in the Quartier Latin.

Georges and Michelle are waiting for me. I can already see Chatouiller hiding behind Aubert's massive effigy. *I can see you, Chatouiller, I am back now!* The women in the square were generous in the cold sunshine when I held out my cup.

I head down the path to Armand to get my things. Tonight, we move to sleep with Le Fleur, who is next to Chopin but more sheltered than his monument, that tall angel with her wings in flight. Chopin will miss us by now. He will be glad to have us near.

I turn left at Seurat. A young couple, cameras draped around their necks like shawls, jostle me rudely as they overtake me. I walk past the side of Hugo's tomb. There is writing on it as far away as this, at the very south end. It is etched *Forever Jim.* And an arrow points. Points ahead and across the trees to the north, far from Chopin. Far from us.

~ 1919 ~
# In Blackbrooke Hall

If I'm going to tell it, then I must tell it from the start, before the house was empty, and before we came to stay there.

The house, called Blackbrooke after the springs that ran behind it, was sizable enough to accommodate the family who built it, a cook, two maidservants, and a groundskeeper. There were fourteen rooms altogether, not including the spacious kitchen. We were told the kitchen was always bustling with activity, with wonderful *haute cuisine* cooked on the great iron stoves: roast lamb and chicken and fresh vegetables from the neighboring farms to feed the many guests who visited the generous and lively family.

Situated among ancient oak trees on the southeastern tip of Long Island, the stone house was built in 1875 by Mr. Willem Van Leuke, a cousin of the renowned painter Pieter Van Leuke, who emigrated from Amsterdam to New York. I imagine he thought the spot beautiful at the time, the great oak's branches surrounding the house like arms, cradling it. But it is the very image of those trees, and their skeletal limbs, that begs me to tell the story that makes my blood run cold even now ...

My cousin Bobby Beresford sat in the driver's seat of the motorcar, its wheels jumping over the rocks, a few snowy patches, and holes in the road.

"If you don't slow down," Miriam nearly shouted over the motor's din, "I'll never see 1919!"

I agreed with our college friend. "Slow down, will you, Bobby?"

"Sit tight, Franny ol' girl." Alex smiled as he put his arm around me in a mock-gallant style, trying to hold us both against the car's jolting. He laughed, looked out the window, and checked the luggage strapped to the running board. "Haven't lost a thing."

"We'll be there in no time," Bobby said. He grinned with excitement in a way that always made me think of him as still a boy, my little cousin who was, really, only a year younger than I. My uncle had bought him the Ford for Christmas and, as it shot noisily past handsoms and coaches, I wondered whether a motorized car for a new toy wasn't a mistake on dear Uncle's part. It was during Christmas dinner that my uncle told us about Blackbrooke Hall of Amagansett. Mr. Templeton, a colleague of his who was the estate agent in charge of the house (it had been empty for years, save the caretaker), suggested the elder Mr. Beresford might take his family on a retreat. Mr. Beresford, in turn, suggested that Bobby and I take some of our college chums instead for the New Year.

"Isn't it awfully dark already?" I asked. "It's always that way this time of year. And all the Christmas cheer gone, too."

"I hope there's a New Year's meal waiting for us," replied my cousin.

"I heard Mr. Templeton tell Uncle he hired a cook."

The car turned onto a path. For a moment, there was nothing but a narrow, dark, tree-lined way, with a dense pine barren to our left. Many of the trees along the path were ravaged and twisted from growing in the pitiless ocean winds. Continuing on for what seemed to me like several more miles, we came upon an old clamdigger driving his cart. The cart was empty, and the old man's hunched back swayed as he drove his horse slowly over the road in front of us.

"Can't he move over and let us pass?" Bobby said, slowing down to a more reasonable speed.

"Maybe we should ask him if we're headed the right way."

Bobby pulled alongside the man, and Alex leaned out the window. "Excuse me, sir. Hello, there! Can you tell us if we're heading toward Blackbrooke Hall?"

The man tugged on his horse's reins. We both came to a halt, the light from our headlamps giving the man a preternatural appearance. "Blackbrooke, yeh say?"

"Yes, that's it. Are we going the right way?"

"Headed the wrong way, if yeh ask me."

"Then we should turn back?"

"If yeh got any sense."

"I'm sorry," said Alex, "I don't understand. We're not gate-crashers, you know. Are we, or are we not, on the road to Blackbrooke Hall?"

"Yeh-ah. Yeh're headed thata way," he said. "And I'd head back where I come from. They'll be no guests at Blackbrooke tonight."

"Well," Bobby said, leaning out his window. "You're wrong about that, but we appreciate the directions. This guy's all wet baloney," he added under his breath.

The old clamdigger pushed his wool cap down on his forehead. "Yeh'd better be taking those women back now. They'll not have 'em at Blackbrooke."

"Thank you," said Alex. "Good night, sir. And a Happy New Year to you."

Bobby pulled the car ahead as we stifled our laughter.

"What a flat tire!"

"He looks a hundred and five."

"He's sore about the weather, that's all. Wishes he were riding in one of these spiffy things."

We continued, the trunks and branches of the trees forming walls and a canopy over us, the air growing colder, rich, and salty. After another stretch, the headlights illuminated a portal, then an old iron gate, shut and locked. Over the gate was a tarnished brass plaque inscribed "Blackbrooke Hall." And beyond it sat the house, dark except for three lit windows. The moon peeked in on its rooftop, then disappeared again under a veil of clouds.

"Can we get in?" asked Miriam.

"There's a lock on the gate," Bobby said.

"Maybe there's a key hanging on the post." A secretary for a law firm in the city, Miriam was a practical girl with a good head on her shoulders and was wholly unafraid of most things. "Are you sure they're expecting us?" she asked. She wrapped her fur tighter around her throat.

My cousin smiled weakly and shrugged.

Just then, I noticed what looked like a lantern up ahead, beyond the locked gate. It bobbed and moved toward us, the flame of the lantern becoming clearer, flickering with the gusts of wind.

"That must be the caretaker." Bobby perked up.

I was glad, though the caretaker's face, lit by a yellowy haze of lantern light, did not comfort me. He was rough-looking, unshaven, wearing a dark, flannel coat and a felt hat shading two unfriendly eyes. Beside him stood his dog, a pale gray husky-like creature whose pale eyes reflected red back at us. I was relieved when the man silently opened the gate and let us through.

Bobby drove the car up the gravel path that led to the front of the house. The air was damp and smelled like fallen leaves, though there were patches of snow all around. The city seemed very far away.

Almost immediately, a man with white hair in butler's attire came out through the massive front door, allowing a large beam of light to illuminate the driveway and car. He was a tall, though slightly stooped fellow, with piercing light eyes and a large, stern nose. He introduced himself as Greyboys and, asking which of the bags belonged to the ladies, proceeded to carry them into the house.

The interior of Blackbrooke Hall was overwhelming. To simply describe it would not do justice to the mysterious feeling I had when first walking through the great house. Electric chandeliers hung like ornate pieces of machinery, their heavy, gilded arms housing sinister-looking brass birds peering down upon worn and ornately patterned Persian rugs. The furniture was an eclectic mix of Mediaeval cathedral pieces and the Victorian brocades and velvets of my parents' childhoods. The walls, when not paneled in mahogany, were covered from floor to ceiling in the deepest red wallpaper with raised velvet *fleurs de lis*. I noticed that a mirror in the front hall had the effect of making one look unusually long. Only seven of the fourteen rooms, Greyboys told us, were in use; the rest had been closed up for years now, their doors locked, the furniture protected by dust covers. The remaining four bedrooms, a sitting room, library, and dining room, were prepared for our visit.

The small staff—the uncanny caretaker we met by the front gate, whose name was James Hale, Greyboys the butler, and Mrs. Dodd, a stout and capable-looking cook—seemed to have gone to great pains to make the house comfortable. Mrs. Dodd had been preparing a feast for our arrival and took special care in preparing for our visit. She had placed fresh hyacinths and poinsettias in the sitting room and library and a large floral centerpiece on the dining room table.

"Say, what do you think of that old butler?" Alex asked as we sat in the dining room, where we were left to ourselves. A hot platter of roast beef was passed around the table with additional large platters of potatoes and spinach soufflé.

"I didn't know he was here," said Bobby. "I thought there was just the cook and the caretaker. Isn't that so, Franny?"

"I don't like that James Hale fellow. He has a mean face."

"You would, too, if you were locked up here all these years," Alex said. He grinned. "I'm sure he's swell when he warms up."

"It is a little ... well, the house, I mean," Bobby said. "It's fantastic. Like a funhouse. The kind at carnivals that have oddly shaped mirrors and ghoulish noises."

"Mr. Hale seems very dedicated to the house," I said. "If that's the way to put it. Uncle's friend Mr. Templeton says he's been here for decades." I handed Miriam the platter of new potatoes sprinkled with rosemary. She inhaled the aroma.

"Well, Mrs. Dodd certainly knows how to cook a New Year's Eve supper," she said. "Scrumptious! Alex, be a darling and pass the champagne, thanks."

We each filled our glasses and gave a toast.

"To a fine and happy new year!" said Bobby. "And good riddance to the War."

"Yes," I echoed. "Happy 1919."

"Here, here! Peace and prosperity for all."

As our glasses clanged against each other like little bells and the excellent French champagne's bubbles tickled my nostrils, I imagined our arrival at Blackbrooke Hall was to begin a lively and relaxing weekend. Later, we retired to the drawing room at Greyboys's suggestion, where a fire blazed and brandy glasses sat next to a carafe on a silver tray.

We sang a rousing chorus of "Auld Lang Syne" sometime around midnight, then played a game of charades in which Alex tried to convince us he was The Red Baron, and Bobby did a passing impression of Chaplin. Finally, we settled down to conversation. While Miriam told me she was planning a trip abroad with her aunt, I noticed Bobby looking at her endearingly and wondered if he was developing a crush on his college friend. We were, all four of us, on the St. Charles Bridge Team and the editorial staff at the University paper. We had seldom enjoyed anything extracurricular separately, yet none of us had ever fixed romantically on each other.

After a while, Bobby and I took a crack at Bezique, first removing the twos, threes, fours, fives, and sixes from two decks we found in a drawer; Miriam toyed at a jigsaw puzzle, while Alex snored softly in a comfortable easy chair next to us, his handsome tweed jacket in a heap at his feet.

 Sometime after two—I remember hearing the chimes of a clock from one of the hallways—we all must have dozed off, me in a high-back chair by the fire, a heart, diamond, and spade still awaiting a club in my hand. I woke with a start to a crashing sound and saw Greyboys standing by the window. I felt a cold blast of air reach me. The fire had all but died. Greyboys's tall silhouette was now like a statue in front of the window; it seemed as if he was looking at me, but I could not see his face.

 "Yes, what do you want?" I asked. At this, Alex stirred. The butler did not reply. "What is it, Greyboys?" I inquired again, half believing I was dreaming or imagining the figure before me.

 "The window was open," he said flatly.

 "But how ...?"

 "Good God, it's cold as ice in here," Bobby moaned. I heard his cards slip to the floor. "Oh, damn. There goes my Sequence."

 "You did not have a Sequence," I retorted, flicking my eight of spades at his chest.

 I roused Miriam, and we all followed the lanky, white-haired gent up the wide staircase, past portraits of deceased Van Leukes and some landscapes masterfully rendered by Pieter Van Leuke, to our rooms.

 I combed and plaited my hair, once again toying with the idea of bobbing the mess of red curls. Then I folded my stockings and pantaloons and put on my dressing gown. As none of the rooms upstairs were wired for electricity, I lit a large pillar candle placed at my bedside for my convenience. I lay in bed, now sober and awake, and looked around in the semi-darkness.

Miriam and I shared a suite, with a door separating our bedrooms. Across the hall, Alex and Bobby's room were, I assumed, adjoined in the same manner. I sat up in the canopy bed, leaning against large down pillows that smelled slightly of old mustiness and mostly of new linen water. The candle on the night table illuminated and shadowed more paintings, paneled walls, and the mantelpiece over the fireplace. On it sat an obtrusive candelabra and curious boxes in varying sizes that made me think of objects in a museum storeroom.

My eyes darted around and rested on a bookshelf. Climbing down from the bed, I selected a book on local whaling ships. I thought about seeing if Miriam was still awake but eventually got caught up in a tale of a captain whose ship had run aground on the rocks off Montauk, though the lighthouse had sounded its horn in warning. Apparently, the captain received news of his wife's death during a stop in Point Judith and had designed to end his miserable life and the lives of his crew before reaching home.

It was somewhere in the middle of this strange story that I heard it. At first, I thought it was the wind. I looked up from my book and over at the window, searching for a ripple in the curtain, a draft, or some indication the window had opened. There was nothing. My candle did not even flicker.

Then I heard it again, a low whistling, like a whispering moan, and realized the sound did not come from outside the room at all, but from inside one of the walls. I should say it was coming from both the wall where the bookshelf stood and the wall adjacent to it where the fireplace stood, because the sound seemed to move from one to the other and back again.

I jumped down from the bed and began to search for a seam in the shelf that might open a hidden door. Then, I became certain that the moaning, growing louder and monstrous, was coming from the fireplace—or perhaps even from inside the chimney.

As I stood before the mantle, I felt a damp blast of air on my legs, as if a horrible ocean wind had blown out from the fireplace. My bones stiffened. I felt the blood leave my face. With all my will, I moved back in the direction of the bed. I had not taken three steps when the howling ceased and I heard the distinct sound of a human cry. The doors across the hall opened and I heard the familiar voices of my cousin and Alex. A second cry came from the bedroom next to mine; it was Miriam, letting out another shriek of fright.

I rushed through the door joining our rooms to find our usually cool-headed Miriam standing at the foot of her bed, clutching the heavy bedspread to her. She was trembling and very pale, and Bobby held her shoulders.

"What happened?" he asked, shaking her a little.

Alex lit a kerosene lamp and stood by the window, where a pane was visibly cracked. "The wind," he said, inspecting the window.

"It wasn't the wind," Miriam whimpered.

I ran to her. "What is it? You're shivering. Sit down."

"The snow ... it was ... I couldn't run. I couldn't move my legs."

"Just a dream," Bobby said to me. He shrugged.

I looked at Bobby and Alex, but their faces revealed neither the fright Miriam obviously experienced nor mine in my own strange encounter, which I had yet to confess to my friends.

"The wind blew that tree branch against the pane and broke it," Alex explained. He pointed, and Bobby nodded in agreement.

"No one's trimmed these trees in years, probably."

"But the snow!" Miriam cried again.

"There, there." I tried to soothe her. "There's no snow. Hasn't been for a week." In a moment, she gained composure. We sat on the edge of the bed. I turned to Bobby.

"Did you hear something before Miriam cried out?" My cousin looked quizzically at me. Alex shook his head when I turned to him. "No sound? Like a caterwaul, or the wind under your door?" I asked.

"Not a sound," said Bobby. "But I was asleep. And happily so," he added with some annoyance.

"Not me," Alex said. "I was up and reading. There are some funny books in my room, and after my doze by the fire earlier, I was wide awake."

"Yes, me too," I said.

"Franny, what did you hear?" Miriam asked. She was almost entirely herself again. I looked at her complexion, returning to a rosy hue.

"Nothing," I said. "Bobby's right. I'm sure it was the wind."

The next morning, we were as usual, cheerful and full of adventure, though I admit that I was preoccupied with the previous night's occurrences. Nevertheless, I brushed it off and concentrated on the present moment.

The breakfast room was really just a small but pretty nook with a half-circle of bay windows off the library. It was bright and had a notable view of the gardens, which sloped to the edge of a high dune and, beyond that, the ocean.

"Say, I really wanted to go out exploring today," Bobby said.

"I wonder if it'll stop," said Alex, referring to the snow that had started up half an hour before. The sky was a dense gray, indicating the snow might continue the rest of the day. It occurred to me that Miriam had mentioned snow as part of the vision she'd had the night before.

"We'll go crazy with nothing to do," Bobby said to me. "I feel cooped up. Pass the jam."

"Bobby, stop being so fidgety," Miriam muttered.

"I'm not!" Bobby shouted. Then he stood up on his chair and began to sing. "To my honey I'll croon love's tune; Honey moon, keep a-shinin' in June; Your silv'ry beams will bring love's dreams; We'll be cuddlin' soon; By the silvery moon ..."

"Someone shut him up before he breaks all the crystal," Alex said. We all laughed.

Bobby continued singing while Miriam pulled on his trouser leg to get him to sit down.

In the midst of this ruckus, Miriam let out a cry of surprise. At the same time, one of the iron-framed window panes cracked loudly, splitting into large pieces, some falling to the floor. Everyone jumped up from their seats and, looking out the window, clearly saw the face of James Hale. His raggedy visage peered in at us from what was fast becoming a snowy white-out.

"Why is that awful man staring at us?" Miriam cried. "What do you want?" she said to James Hale through the window. Hale's dog, pale fur bristling in the cold, barked loudly and repeatedly, his tail hanging low. "Can't you see that a pane has been broken? Why are you standing there?" Miriam demanded. "Do something, will you?"

"He can't hear you," Alex said, ringing for Greyboys.

By this time, Mr. Hale had fled. We fully expected him to appear again at the door to the library, but only Greyboys came in to inspect the window in question. After examining it, he proclaimed that the glass must have had a hairline crack, and Mr. Hale had perhaps tapped on the frame to get our attention.

"He's been out chopping wood," Greyboys said in his usual flat tone. His strong nose twitched slightly. "He was no doubt trying to come into the house through the back and desired you to open the door."

We were all silent for a moment, each of us looking to the others to confirm this unlikely explanation.

"Say, Greyboys," said Alex dryly. "You didn't happen to hear anything unusual last night, did you?"

"No, sir."

"No, Greyboys? No moaning sound? The sound of a loud and sickly cat, maybe?"

I leaned forward. I could see Miriam eyeing me.

"No, sir," replied Greyboys. "Perhaps it was the wind."

"No," said Alex. "No, not the wind."

"Sir?"

"But you heard someone scream?"

Greyboys looked blankly at Alex. "I don't believe I did, sir."

"Our Miriam here was scared silly. One of the windows in her room behaved in much the same way as this little one did here. I stuffed my handkerchief in it so the room wouldn't freeze."

"I will tell Mr. Hale to fix both panes at once. You'll excuse me, now." He turned to leave, then paused. "It's best to stay in today. The wind has shifted. It's coming from the northeast."

My cousin made us a blazing fire in the library, where we sat for the remainder of the day. Mrs. Dodd provided us with mouthwatering cakes and hot chocolate.

I noticed Alex in an easy chair by the fireplace, writing letters. I took my stationery and pulled up a chair alongside his. I decided it was time I write to my mother's sister in Rhode Island and propose Miriam and I might share the apartment she owned in Manhattan. My mother had mentioned over Christmas that Aunt Permelia barely used it, and Miriam and I were keen on working and living in the city. I took out my pen, leaning my stationery on a big book on my lap. I paused and looked at Alex. When I looked down at his lap, it was not a letter he was writing; he was drawing. He had repeatedly rendered a rectangular shape, one-dimensional in design.

"What is that?"

He stared blankly at me, as if he was confused by the question. I touched the corner of his page with my finger, and when I did so, he took my hand in his. His countenance became one of fear.

"What is it?" I asked. Looking down at the drawing, I could now see there was a smaller, thin, rectangular piece attached to the larger shape. It was as if it were a handle to ... but why would Alex have drawn, in what was surely an unconscious gesture, a razor?

"Alex?"

"I—I don't know." His voice rose to an uneasy tone.

"What's all the commotion over there?" Bobby asked.

"Why, Alex is drawing pictures of very sharp weapons," said Miriam, who was, by now, looking over his shoulder.

"Not so. It's a shaving device," he murmured.

The room itself began to take on that same uncertain quality the breakfast room had hours ago, the way my own room had the previous night. As Bobby got up from his chair by the fire and crossed the room, surely to have a look at the drawing and poke fun at his nervous friends, the lights in the room fluttered, then went out.

"Oh, perfect!" Bobby exclaimed. "Now what?"

"I think we should ring for Greyboys," I said.

"He'll be in soon enough, the old ghoul."

"I'll get a lamp. Bobby, put more wood on the fire." And with that, Miriam started out of the room.

"There is no more wood. Miriam, wait! I think we should stay together."

But it was too late. My cousin's protests could not keep Miriam from doing the practical thing, which was to search for some means of light. In a moment, the electricity returned with a flicker, though it was weakened and the lights were dimmed. Alex, Bobby, and I stood blinking at one another, then went out the door to find Miriam. Though we looked all around the main floor, we could not find her.

"Where is that blasted Greyboys when you need him?" Alex glanced around another corner. "It feels as if the whole house has been emptied. Listen—I don't hear that blasted dog, either."

The three of us proceeded up the stairs. We checked our rooms for Miriam and met out in the hallway.

"I don't know where she could be," said Bobby.

Looking down the long corridor, I noticed a door at the end of it.

"That's the door leading to the rest of the second-floor rooms," said Alex. "Why would Miriam be in there?"

Bobby tried the door. "It's locked. It won't open."

"That doesn't mean it's locked." Alex pushed against the door. "The doorknob turns; it's just ... a little ... stuck."

It gave way and opened with a loud creak into a narrow hallway, off of which were other doors. I opened the first one, and we entered a large, abandoned sitting room, its furniture cloaked in dust cloths. A huge gilded mirror, cloudy with age, reflected our images. Alex took a candle from a mantle and ignited the wick with his lighter. He then led us to another door, which opened into a bedroom, its furniture also covered. Alex took my hand and the three of us moved forward.

"There's another door, there," Bobby pointed. "I feel like I'm in a maze."

We practically fell through this doorway to find ourselves in what looked like a kind of artist's studio, a converted bedroom. In it, there stood an old easel made of strong wood and of excellent craftsmanship, along with numerous trays of oil paints and water-wash palettes, a chaise lounge, two stools, a work table, and a wardrobe with an old padlock on its doors. The room was swept and scrubbed clean. No drop cloths, nor dried splatters of paint, nor canvases.

"Well, this is odd," I heard my cousin say. He was poking around at the various objects and furnishings.

At the main entrance to the room, out in the hall, stood Miriam, looking down at the threshold in shock.

"Miriam! Where have you been?" I cried.

Alex held out his arm to stop me from rushing toward her. "What is it, Miriam?" he called.

Miriam, seemingly transfixed by the ground in front of her, whispered, "It's evil. Look at it—it's terrible and evil."

We moved forward and looked down at the threshold. A chill of pure fear came over me as I beheld what I did. The door, opening into the room about halfway, was thick and heavy mahogany. The light from the hallway where Miriam stood did not pour into the darkened room in which we stood the way light naturally would, but instead, the darkness from the room poured out into the lit hallway, casting a shadow over Miriam's feet.

"My God, look at it," she cried terribly.

Alex rushed forward, stopping in the doorway and looking closely at the sight. He ventured onto the shadow itself, the dark form remaining unchanged. Alex's shadow did not appear beyond the shadow of the doorway. "Stay there, Miriam," he cautioned. "Come on, you two," he motioned to my cousin and me.

Following Alex's lead, we stepped over the threshold. I instantly felt a chill in doing so, not just from my own fear, but from an icy draft that hit me straight on as I passed through the doorway. I shuddered. "Did you feel that?"

"Yes," said Bobby.

"Now we're going downstairs," said Alex, "and we're going to find Greyboys and find out once and for all ..."

"The closet." Miriam's voice was a mere whisper.

"What's that, dear?" I put my arm around her.

She pointed back to the room. "There's something about the closet."

"Look, I think she means that dresser in there," said Bobby.

"It's a wardrobe," I corrected. "And it's locked. Didn't you see? And yet ..." I had to agree with Miriam. It was peculiar that, so many years after a family ceased to live in a house, it should remain locked up.

"Please, let's just go downstairs. *Please*," I said.

At my outburst, Alex and Bobby went back into the room.

I could not bring myself to look at that dreadful shadow that lay before me as I attempted to comfort Miriam, nor could I stand there listening to the howling of the wind and the sound of it beating the snow against the windows and exterior of the house. It was maddening. I drew Miriam closer to me and brought her quickly into the room. Alex and Bobby, who had rested their candle on the floor, were forcing the lock open with the flat end of an artist's hammer.

The lock broke. When the doors swung open, we saw canvases leaning against each other, each no bigger than two or three feet wide. Bobby and Alex began pulling the pictures out and leaning them against the wall so we could have a look at them. I held the candle up to each one, and the faces of persons long gone stared back at me. They were portraits, mostly from the shoulders up, of various ladies and gentlemen in formal attire.

"Say, do you notice anything peculiar about these?" asked Bobby.

"Come on now, pal, there's nothing scary about a bunch of old paintings. We're just letting our imaginations get the best of us." Alex sighed, relaxing against the wardrobe door.

"Yes," said Miriam softly. She was beginning to collect herself. "They're just portraits."

"But there is something," I ventured. "Their expressions." I moved the candle back and forth along the faces. Forlorn, empty, lifeless. "It's almost as if ..." my voice trailed off.

It's almost as if they were dead. I dared not say it, for saying it would imply I could even imagine how such a gruesome act could be accomplished.

Miriam began to whimper. Alex shined his candle back into the wardrobe, and he and Bobby began removing boxes and objects wrapped in cloth.

"What's this? A leather pouch?"

"It's a shaving kit."

But the kit was nothing more than a razor and sharpener; the rest of the kit was empty. Even in candlelight, I could see Alex's face go white. It was the exact instrument he had sketched in the library. The kit dropped to the floor just as Miriam let out a cry.

"Look there!"

Dangling out of the wardrobe was the skeletal remains of a very small hand, its ring finger caught on the edge of the wardrobe's frame.

It was then that we heard a loud crack and turned to see the limbs of an imposing oak tree, like skeletal fingers themselves, scraping the suddenly broken window of the room. The finger-like shadows of the branches played over and smacked against the pane, as if crying out for us to let them in.

We ran out into the hall and down the grand staircase.

We did not find Greyboys, nor Mrs. Dodd or James Hale. Once in the bright light of the kitchen, we agreed to attempt to make it through what had become a true nor'easter in Bobby's car and send for our things later.

The boys threw a rug over our laps in the backseat. With some difficulty, the car made it through the storm, and we found that, once we were on the main road to town, the snow lessened. We arrived safely at Uncle's house on Fifth Avenue sometime before dawn.

"Listen to this," Bobby said. He held one of the many books and documents we had gathered the following weekend from an archive that specialized in area homes and architecture. Our selection was made from their records of East End houses.

My cousin, Miriam, Alex, and I sat comfortably in my uncle's library. We had not told anyone about our stay that New Year's weekend. We ourselves had begun to wonder if what we had experienced was not in fact some figment of our imaginations, and it was Alex's idea to research the house and find out all we could.

"Listen to this bit here," Bobby said. He bent over his book. "The house was built by a cousin of the famous Dutch painter, Pieter Van Leuke. This Willem Van Leuke, as it turns out, was a local representative and had his eye on the U.S. Senate. He lived in Blackbrooke Hall with his wife, Fiona, daughter Beatrix, and son, William."

"And Mr. Van Leuke's brother," interrupted Miriam. "It says so here. There's a brief accounting of him in this old journal, written by an acquaintance of the family. He was an artist, just like the cousin Pieter."

We looked through more books, drawings of the house that revealed that it was slightly lopsided in design, and which did not show the extra rooms on the second floor. "Perhaps they were additions," Bobby suggested hopefully.

It was in another journal, a book of days and diary notes, that I found what we had been seeking. I read aloud from this diary of sorts, an accounting by a young woman, apparently a schoolmate of the elder Van Leuke sister:

Groton, Connecticut
12 October, 1890
> *How gruesome is that which I know now! That which I can scarcely bring pen to paper to tell, yet I must, or else burst with the knowledge of abominations. Poor, poor Beatrix! My dear friend may never recover. I must tell it as she did, leaving no details un-turned so that, in this confession, I may perhaps rid her of these things that haunt her still. These things that, even as I write this from our warm and sheltering room at our good Christian school, make her toss and cry out in her sleep.*
> *I have been there by ferry, to that cursed house Blackbrooke, once myself three Christmases ago, when we were not thirteen and merely acquaintances through our father's business dealings. Mr. Van Leuke was so fond of entertaining guests, and giving parties and dinners. I found it most agreeable when I stayed. Beatrix's mother was a gregarious woman who loved to oversee the kitchen as the servants concocted the wonderful dishes we dined on. The younger brother, William, bless his soul, was also an agreeable sort, though timid and frail, and one to hang about his sister in a strangely frightened way, which she did not seem to mind at all. So the house and its owners I liked well and good. And yet, even then, during my father's and my*

short stay, I could feel the evil that lurked there, under the surface, protected by these good people.

I occasioned to meet only once during my stay, the other Mr. Van Leuke—Beatrix's Uncle Jan, the younger brother to her father. I came across him accidentally when I took a wrong turn on the way to my room. He was coming out of his painting studio. He brushed past me rudely, his coat tails splattered with paint and smudged with dust, his hair unkempt. He did not even look at me, though I had been told that he could be charming. He was the eccentric talent, the genius of the family. Outside his studio door lay his dog, a pale gray sled-dog with equally pale eyes that seemed to bore through me as he glared at me.

And now to the tale I have avoided with these details. It was during our break-term, Christmas and New Year's of this year past, that it happened. Beatrix and I had already spent a term together and got along famously, for I loved her intelligence and sweet ways, and the way in which she so carefully watched over the younger girls at our school.

I had written to Beatrix just after Christmas and had planned to call on her and her family, when I received a strange letter. In it, she made the usual small talk of holiday festivities and gifts she had received. But at the end of it, she confided in me that she was worried about returning to school in January, mainly because she did not want to leave her little brother. I believed she alluded to his fragile and sickly nature and sympathized with her concern.

Had I known what really occurred under that great roof, under the watchful arches of those huge trees, and the auspices of Mr. Willem Van Leuke, I would have persuaded my father to help little William into the boy's academy nearby.

It was a cold, snowy night, the first of January. There had been no New Year's banquet, no weekenders at the stroke of midnight, no festivities. Beatrix's father had become, quite suddenly, reluctant to have any guests at the house. Beatrix was reading in the library. Young William had sat by her most of the evening until it was time for bed. Beatrix tucked William in and retired to her room with its shelves full of books and cozy fireplace and mantle.

It was somewhere around two o'clock that she heard it—the cry of a child. She ran to her window and threw it open, believing the sound coming from outside in the storm. She listened carefully, at first unsure as, the way the house had been constructed, sound traveled strangely. She ran next door to William's room and, on finding her brother was not in his bed, she donned her cloak and boots and set out into the storm to find him.

Out into the blistering wind and snow she went, fearing he had taken to walking in his sleep, as he had been known to sometimes do. She heard a pitiful moan, then, as she was coming round the side of the house. Her eyes followed what her ears had heard, up the big oak tree they were so fond of climbing, to the window whose branches it touched. The window of her uncle's room. She could not make it round the house in time; she had to try and get to the window. Climbing like she did as a little girl during springtime, she made her way up the trunk and out along the largest branch, all the while the child's scream growing dimmer in the howling wind. Gripping the window ledge with her frostbitten hands, she peered into the window.

Can I describe what she saw? I only know what she herself confided in me. There stood the uncle, a blank canvas on the easel, his face flushed with excitement. William was slumped, lifeless, in a chair before him, his throat slashed. Beatrix screamed. Her hand reached for him and broke the glass pane, causing her uncle to look up. The pupils of his eyes constricted so that their pale irises glowed furiously at her. In his hand he held something that he waved in her direction, ordering her to get down.

Once down from the tree, Beatrix made her way in the storm to a neighboring farm, some two miles past the Van Leuke property. It was there that she collapsed on the doorstep, and the authorities were notified. When they came to the house early that morning, the body of young William had disappeared. It was later in the day that it was recovered. It had been stuffed up into the chimney in Beatrix's room. The poor boy was missing a hand, his right, and it is assumed that, in the struggle, he had reached out to protect himself, his uncle severing the hand.

Jan Van Leuke fled Blackbrooke Hall and was found weeks later in New York City through an art collector who purchased three of the hideous paintings, not knowing what he had acquired. You see, it was not the regular sort of paintings the uncle did. For he would paint portraits of people, often the very guests who had been to the house, by some grotesque method of murder by a sharp instrument, thereby drawing the blood out and using it as pigment for some of the colors. He would then lock the body in his room, propped up in its portrait position, and paint the ghastly corpse. When he was through, he disposed of the body by burying it under the trees around the property.

It was during this winter that his elder brother, Beatrix's father, became suspicious of his *brother's abominations. He could not bring himself, as he should have—for these events unfolded in his own home!—to have his brother locked away properly. So, in an act of cowardice and grievous judgment, he ordered that no guests be received. He thought that by preventing victims from entering the house, there would be no victims.*

The elder Mr. Van Leuke was ruined. The house was shut down, as no one would buy it. The school here has taken pity on poor Beatrix, as had my own father, who pays half her expenses.

Ah, now she is stirring again, dear, sweet friend! I pray nightly that she receives some peace, if only in sleep. That God would give her that much would be little compensation for the evil He allowed to enter her young life ...

I stopped, the diary open in my lap. "Do you think—" I whispered; but Miriam quickly, almost imperceptibly, shook her head.

"Don't say another word," she said, her voice trembling.

Beside her, Alex and Bobby sat motionless, their eyes fixed on mine.

~ 1883 ~
The Dream

An excerpt from the novel *The Crewel Wing*.

In my dream, I found myself with my sister, the two of us walking arm in arm in a large and bustling city. Outwardly ordinary and harmless, the moment was a trick. Just before we strolled the avenue—before I noticed I was with Meg—I could have been in any number of places, different places, so that I could not tell whether I was in this dream—the one I feared—or another. Then, there was the walk, the wide High Street with its well-dressed men and women sauntering, the entrance to the park, the bare trees and, worst of all, the black horse.

    It was a nightmare that followed me from place to place, like an old bed cap one pulls out of a drawer when settling down for the night. On the eve of the wedding, I awoke, fretful, in our room at the hotel, my sister sleeping soundly beside me as usual. I couldn't sleep, then, for wondering what would happen on nights like this when she was gone.

    "If Mother were here," Meghan said to me in the morning, a kind of questioning sigh in her voice. She was draped and bustled in cream lace, petite and fair. Her delicacy made it easy for me to see her slightly swollen belly pushing against the tight corset, and I wondered if anyone else noticed.

"You do not even remember her, dearest," I said in a tone that was not so kind. Then I kissed Meg's cheek, for it is I who usually held my tongue.

Like Father, my little sister was the free thinker. "I do remember her," she muttered back at me. Her mouth was curled in a smile, though, and her dainty limbs clung to me with surprising force when we embraced.

For most people, life happens in one place, a handful of common events etched deeply into an otherwise plain and familiar world. For us, life did not happen in any one place. We had been so many places that I couldn't even remember some of them. Truly, there were only a few events that stood out; memories carved in jagged, chaffed lines. My mother dying in her bed was one. Though even this was muddled, its edges blurring between beginning and end, past and present. Between what I actually witnessed and what I had to imagine.

But, I told myself, *I must not think on that now.* Now, I had to make certain Meghan's train was lifted as we entered the church, that the petals in my basket were still nestled safely, waiting to be scattered before her feet.

Afterward, like always, there were no good-byes. We did not have time for them. I didn't cry or cling desperately. Nor did I bounce up and down clapping my hands in excited little bursts of happiness as Meg and Peter rushed from the church under a shower of rice and coins. Father and I boarded our rented coach even before the couple ascended theirs. My little Meghan stood on the cobblestoned street, hanging onto her groom's arm while reaching for me with her free hand. My fingers folded around hers, and then we were pulled apart. Our bright red calash began to move.

"Meg," I called. I felt I had something left to tell her, but didn't know what it was exactly. "You stupid girl," was one thing I wanted to say; or, "You clever girl." I reached out of the open carriage for her one last time. "Meg!" My voice was now a surprising shout.

"Good luck and God bless, young newlyweds," Father interrupted. It was he, and not a coachman, who was in the driver's seat of our carriage. He, who oiled the old leather to make it shine before the ceremony.

"Care well for my Meghan, lad," he cried to Peter. He waved and laughed as he snapped the reins. Then he exclaimed, to the low, grey sky more than to his remaining daughter, "Our new adventure has begun. The future awaits!"

We cleared the stony, winding village where Meg was settled for good. I watched my father's back. His blue velvet waistcoat pulled against his jolly, round frame as he drove.

"Good-bye to these dark, cold Lancashire days," he cried. "Spring? What spring is this? We'll have summer now, Claire, in the South."

I yearned for these words and the sound of his warm, laughing voice, even as he spoke them. Even as I listened and did not believe him.

"At the sea—yes! The coast will be our holiday," my father decided.

"I suppose the sea would ..."

"—What is that? Speak up, my dear, you have been a mouse with a toad's rasping voice this whole day."

"It is only noon, Father."

"You are parched from last night's champagne—as am I, ha! A wedding feast fit for the Queen, was it not? Fine bubbly is always best from crystal."

"It was only ale. The wedding dinner is still to come."

"But never mind, tea in a fragrant meadow will restore your musical voice in no time. I shall sit you on the Macintosh square. No, no, I insist on it. Standing will do my legs good. You must not catch a chill with your sore throat. Now where shall we pull over? Let's ride on a bit. I feel the air growing milder as we go. Wretched Lancashire!"

"It is not my throat. It is just that Meg is gone." I suddenly noticed my hand was circling my neck, pressing on skin beneath gold: a large, men's ring dangling from a chain.

"Look there. I knew the sun would break through. Do you see? To the south, it is clear. Do not think on the clouds when there is sun ahead. Dear girl, this is most unlike you."

"Forgive me, Father," I managed. The moment was, I admit, unusual, for I rarely ruminated on departures or arrivals.

A little over a week later, we were sufficiently south, but not a bit near the coast. We had, in fact, made it to Cornwall. There, fog encased the normally mild coastline like a swarm of intrusive ghosts for the entire two-day stay. Then it was east by gig to Laverstock, near Salisbury.

From there, we headed farther east to London for just one night. The squalid chaos of the city never brought my father much luck. I hated London, even if this time we did stay in a nice-enough rooming house. I met our brief delay with shut eyes and gritted teeth. I'd only ever spent a handful of days in the City, and all of these recollections included the sight or sound of something ghastly: the frail-looking climbing boys employed by the chimney sweeps scaling the soot-covered rooftops in their tatty shoes; the mangled hands of a neighbor child, a little girl who helped feed her parents by scrambling under machinery to retrieve cotton bobbins; the once-pretty women standing on a corner selling matchbooks, flowers, their bodies.

From the city, we made a kind of snaking half-moon around the countryside, settling, as we always did, with a random turn. There was a village called Pettypoole that sat innocuously on the border of the Thames Valley and the ancient limestone hills of Glouceshire, and Father was looking for a place to rent there. We should have been looking nearer a big town with more opportunities and less familiarity among its people, and I was puzzled as to why we were not. There was no one I could confer with now about Father's plans now that Meg was not here.

I missed Meg's presence as a weaver might miss a finger. I should have been glad we didn't have to worry about her. Her husband, like his father before him, was a head nurseryman for a large estate's gardens. She would probably never go hungry again. And her child, too, would be well-fed and live in a house owned by Peter's family. I suspected the baby would arrive in just five months' time. At least I'd seen the small change in Meg before we were parted: her plumpness, the sense of awe and fear in her eyes, her almost wild laughter and silent swoons of nausea that no one but I noticed. Perhaps it was wrong that I didn't tell her I knew she was with child before her wedding. Or told Father. Then again, no. I would have done almost anything for him, but I wouldn't have done that.

In truth, I felt myself annoyed at my sister now. We said we'd write often to each other, but I knew we wouldn't always get each other's letters in a timely fashion. The morning of the wedding, she snuck a letter into my traveling bag.

> *You must care for yourself, now, Claire. You can't continue to live this gypsy life of Father's. I know, now, how wonderful it is to really belong ...*

The letter pressed against me from inside my dress pocket, gnawing and insistent. I truly did not know what she meant. I'd never belonged to anything else than what I already knew.

And for the time being, my concern was with the road before us. Cotswolds' roads were difficult to negotiate, we were discovering. They collected water from the flooding canals when it rained. There was a lot of mud. It slapped up the side of the dog-cart onto my dress.

"Steady, boy!" Father called out to our horse as we tried to guide him away from a deep, sodden tract. "Steady up the bank—that's it, well done."

I turned in my seat to check on our cargo strapped beneath a tarpaulin.

"Look up, Claire. The trees are bursting," Father remarked. "How glorious that first vibrant glow of nature is."

"Yes, Father."

It was very pretty the way the little bright green florets speckled the branches low and high. The way Yellow Hats and Purple Perfume were sprouting along roadway, path, and garden. Of course, if I didn't agree, I might have said yes to Father anyway.

At Meghan's wedding, my father had declared praises for the beginnings of bright Gipsy Hyacinth in Peter's family's garden and for the China Roses in Meg's bouquet. Father always called those flowers by their proper names, which, he said, were exceptional as they were and didn't need embellishment. The Yellow Hats and Purple Perfume we passed were, I think, really daffodils and something else I didn't know the name of. I knew nothing of proper gardening, except whatever Father told me of it. I had not sunk my fingers into the earth since I was a child and hadn't cultivated a garden long enough as an adult to figure out which weedy-looking plant was which before we had to move away from it.

"Here we are; here we are, Claire," Father said with delight.

Having made it through the aqueous mess of roads that ran to and from Pettypoole, we reached a fair on the outskirts of town.

"Today will be a fine day, indeed, I can sense it." He patted my knee and hauled himself down to pull our horse to the watering tent. By the end of the day, he would sell the gelding and the cart, but not before he also sold some of his wares.

We hitched up to a tree on the very edge of the fairgrounds. I patted the horse's neck. He was a sweet one, light red-brown with a dark mane and a soft disposition, but the feel of his taut, strong hide reminded me of my dream. I felt uneasy as we put the back of the wain down and covered the floor with some dark blue velvet. The heels of my boots sank into the spongy earth as I picked bits of wet hay out of the platform's rusty hinges.

I helped my father set up several silver porridge bowls, serving platters, a tea set, and cutlery that he obtained while in London. Before long, he was working very hard to convince another dealer to take the pieces off his hands.

"And they were taken from Versailles, when?" the dealer asked again. He owned a covered van filled with treasures himself, from one of Catherine the Great's riding skirts to a palace urn belonging to the great Chinese Emperor Ch'ien-lung, whose authenticity he fiercely attested to.

"It is a story filled with history," said Father. He spoke with an appealing combination of complaisance and solemn ceremony. "The bowls were fashioned long before France's great Revolution. They belonged to Antoinette's mother, made for her one-hundred-twenty years ago. Do you see the Austrian markings? The stamp of the maker? Well, we know what happened to her poor daughter Antoinette." Father paused, shaking his head. He brightened quickly. "It was on our tour of the Continent that I came across them quite by accident. You know how two young ladies will shop!"

The man chuckled at this. "Two daughters? Oh my, oh my."

"Whilst in Vienna, I noticed this lovely set, returned to its place of origin. But, of course, both of my girls are very much attached to their grandmothers' china and silver, of which they each have sets, so in the end, we have no real use for these …"

My father did not wear the monger's colorful uniform of long cord waistcoat, colorful silk scarf, and silk hat. He was always dressed as a country gentleman. Today, he wore a bottle-green spencer over a tweed vest that hugged his round belly, and green wellies. A rustic but elegant tartan scarf was thrown casually around his neck, where his full white beard gleamed. His eyes crinkled below the brim of his tweed cap. He looked as if he has just finished his morning walk to his stables in preparation for an afternoon hunt.

"Look, here," he pointed to the smooth edge of a bowl. "Such exquisite craftsmanship. 'Tis a pity to let them go," he added with a sigh. "Are you certain, Claire, that you wish to part with them? No, you are right, there's little need with such beautiful and sentimental sets at home."

The dealer nodded, inspecting the pieces carefully as a jeweler might a diamond. The two of them—the dealer and Father—were now deftly colluding in the ruse.

My father handed me a soup terrine. It was, in fact, of good craftsmanship, though I highly doubted it once belonged to that famously beheaded French queen. I was used to these little lies by now, even the ones at my own expense. But I did not like them. They made me nervous, setting me to keep track of which tales were told to whom.

I was beginning to dread finding a new place to stay. We were going to rent a flat, Father told me last night, until we found our perfect house. But I had lost hope that we would settle for good in any place. More likely, there would be rented manor houses abandoned by bankrupted nobles, with leaky ceilings and clogged chimney flues. Or unused summer cottages with once-glorious, neglected gardens, and no gas for light or coal for heat. That was the truth. No tale of Father's could tell it differently.

"And this sugar bowl. Claire?" Father cleared his throat, holding out his hand.

I handed him the bowl, smiling at the dealer. I tried not to think about how my dress was still edged with mud from the morning's ride. There were olive-green flowers with purple centers scattered about the muslin. That morning, Father told me that the pattern on the cloth made my brown hair seem darker and brighter, my eyes more green. The dress was the outcome of an exchange made with a cousin of Peter's on the muggy day of the wedding, and I wore it almost every day since, be it warm or cool.

My wardrobe changed by exchange or circumstance; unpredictable as our living situations. In truth, I thought it great fun to have, so unexpectedly, a new fine dress or cloak. Though I found it difficult to keep up with what was considered current fashion. What we could afford to clothe me in at any given time did not always reflect a need for the coolest summer dress or warmest coat. I didn't always look as other young ladies did. My bustle was sometimes not high enough, my hem not long enough. My bodice a bit too short or too long. My hat brim was often too wide or too narrow, wool when it should have been straw; my duster woven linen when it should have been tweed.

My father nearly settled on a deal involving a box of ivory-handled cutlery. "Ah, now here is a lovely set indeed. But what should a widower like myself do with another when I have four more at home that our poor scullery maid must polish weekly? Though two will be for my eldest daughter's dowry, of course, as they have been in my family for many decades."

"Is she to marry soon?" asked the dealer congenially.

"Soon, yes, sooner than I would like." He smiled at me as if this was true. "My youngest has found happiness already: a young lord met on our trip abroad. What romance it all was!"

He winked to give me permission, and I slipped away to walk through the festival. My father's voice followed me at first, then faded as I strolled on.

I didn't mind fairs if they were in the country, like this one. But they could be dull after a while and required long hours. Other people—ordinary people—seemed to like such festivals, thinking them quaint or enchanting. The ladies fancied themselves Guinevere for a day, adventuring around, enjoying all the exotic and ancient things, before returning to their comforts. For me, it meant being in the thick of Father's gambles.

To get to these events, we often needed to travel a good distance, and that meant I had to plan ahead where to get our supper for later in the evening. I knew I ought to purchase some plum duff and pasties before the stands were sold out. I had a ha'pence in my pocket, but Father was still trying to get more out of that dealer. It would have been better if he gave me another two for a wedge of cheese as well. I dared not ask him. He would give me what he wanted. Or not. To ask would make him secret away more earnings to spend later at the pub.

Father had visited the little village's pub already, with its long, sticky tables and benches, its fetid smell of puddled ale and overcooked lamb. The Lantern, it was called. Inside, people laughed and spoke at full volume, and after sunset, the light inside was dim and warm. But that wasn't enough to make it appealing to me; I wondered if tonight Father would spend all the money he made at The Lantern and then have nothing for tomorrow's supper.

Last night, we, or rather, I slept in our cart. We had sheltered it under a large tree in a field near a crumbling stone church, its stone walls embraced by vines. I lay on a mattress of loose straw on wood, the canvas tarpaulin draped over a single wood brace. I stared at the soiled underside of the cloth. The covering appeared a low and shadowy sky above me, the cart's platform a hard nest. Father was not back from the pub yet. I was left to fend for myself. He must have forgotten, again, that Meghan was not with us; with me.

Around me, endless land stretched out emptily, harmlessly. The only possible threat: the silent spirits lurking around the old stone bethel. Even their presence I doubted, though I didn't much like the look of the mossy structure in the indefinite shadows of night. There was also the stale smell and equally indistinguishable ceiling above me. That seemed worse than anything.

I climbed out, taking the velvet cloth with me, and curled up in the long grass near the sleeping horse. His back rose and fell with a sigh as I moved closer to his warm ribcage. I looked up at the sky. The moon was shadowed every minute or so by thick, fast-moving clouds.

It wasn't long before the quietude of the gelding's company turned into the rattle and terror of the high black carriage; the dangerous gallop of the black horse. I felt my sister clutching my arm, her fingers painfully imprinting white into pink. I tried standing up against the lurching, tried reaching around the driver on his perch to grab the reins. The horse galloped out of control, barely missing lampposts, bare trees, and a few people walking through the dormant, grassy knolls of a park. His hoofs, thundering against stones, cracked and bled, splattering red on the path.

I awoke at dawn to the echoing thunder of a far-off shot, a gamer's aim taking hold of some small animal. My father's figure approached from the other direction. He waved a jug of milk at me.

I thought, as I now made my way around the fair, that even while Mother was alive, we rarely stayed put. I was born in gloomy York, Meg in hazy Brighton. There were two years in London, in a cramped flat on the south side. I was very young and didn't remember it well, and I was glad for it.

The years on the farm in Suffolk were of a different sort altogether. I was nearly twelve when we arrived. I still remembered fields streaked with beams of sunshine against a blue-grey marbled sky and a hiding place I made in the limbs of an enormous tree. The farm belonged to Mother's sister Aileen, a childless widow who died of a cancer in her womb at forty years and who left Mother the farm with ten acres, a herd of healthy goats, and three horses.

Mother's rosy face beamed as she puttered about the house, unpacking our things, her chestnut-brown hair, like mine, framing her face in ringlets as she worked. As she leaned down and stood up repeatedly, her back remained beautifully straight, her corset stiff and neat against her small waist. "We shan't need this again," she said, handing me a milk crate of hay in which some things had been packed. Her voice quivered slightly through her smile, like a breath of hope being released in small portions. Hope and grief, intermingled. Her sister was dead, but my mother's life, through Aileen's farm, was finally blooming before her.

"Take this out to the barn and feed it to the goats." She laughed softly but merrily, handing me the hay. She sent me off with little Meg clinging to my dress.

It was while we lived on the farm that we continued raising goats for milk and wool successfully. Then, one morning, we awoke to find all eighteen of the healthy white and brown animals gone, traded by Father at a tavern for eight bushels of Dutch tulip bulbs. Mother locked herself in her room for two days. I could hear her long, despondent sobs and moans from a cupboard under the stairs where I hid with Meg, my hands over my ears.

The bulbs, not preserved properly at the start, rotted in the cold, damp English earth. Next, Father tried his hand at growing grapes for wine, "the finest vines to make the most sought-after vintage in all of Britain," he boasted. After two sour crops, he settled on a clerk's job at a bank in the larger town nearest us. But it was too late. Mother, sallow-faced and chilled, had been coughing spots of blood into her handkerchief for over a month.

I entered her room one afternoon to find the curtains drawn, her face almost the same shade as the dull, white sheets. I knelt down beside the bed, taking her hand. "Mama, what is it?"

"Is that Aileen?"

"It is Claire, Mama. Aunt Aileen is dead."

"Of course. Mind the horses, then, in her place. Father must not know she is gone."

"We have but one mare, Mama."

"I'm sorry, dearest. Do we not have Ebony?"

"He was sold, Mama."

"I'm confused. And the goats?"

I hesitated. "They are gone, too. Remember?"

"Yes, he has lost them. And me."

"Please sit up, Mama. Sit up. Your cough is worse with lying down."

"My dearest, my dearest," she kissed my hand over and over, her lips cracked and scabbed. "What will become of the nannies? Make certain they nurse the kids, Claire, make sure of it."

"Please, Mama. The goats are long gone. Let me fetch Father."

"No. Stay with me. Stay with me, Aileen. Father will be home. Tell Mother that Father will be home soon."

I did not have it in me to tell her again that her sister and my grandparents were dead. I thought that so long as she did not see them herself, visiting her in some shadowlike fashion, then she would be all right. I stayed with her through the afternoon and night just to make certain, my knees bruised on the hard, cold floor.

The next morning, I met a boy I knew named Will at the stone wall that ran alongside our property. He was sixteen, the son of our neighbor to the south who was a silversmith whose fingertips were always black. Will's fingertips were also tinted from helping his father and learning his trade. We were talking, leaning our elbows on the wall, and I almost forgot that Mother was still in her room looking ghostly. I think I even laughed a little with him.

Will climbed over the wall to help me carry a bag of grain back to the barn. There, he stole a kiss from me. The straw under our feet smelled rich and sweet, and Will's mouth tasted of salt and warm bread. The skin on his hands was rough, but when he ran his fingers along my face and kissed me with his soft, boyish mouth, the contrast made my back arch as if tickled.

We kissed again until we heard his father calling for him. He ran out of the barn, but not before smiling at me, leaving me flushed and leaning against the doorway. The next day, my mother was sent to hospital five miles away. A week later, she was dead. I never saw Will again. After a time, I forced myself not to think of him.

I never actually viewed my mother in her coffin. She was sent off to get well but never came home. Father went almost every day to see her. He seemed so hopeful she was being cured, telling us we wouldn't recognize her when she returned as she would be looking so well and rosy by then, her hair longer and thicker than before. "She'll be mistaken for your sister, Claire," he said with a chuckle.

The day after her death, Father packed Meghan and me up. He'd already had our mother buried in the sanatorium's churchyard without us. At the time, he said he thought it best we not remember her that way: in the cold ground surrounded by others who had fallen from some terrible disease or another. He was "a Practicalist," he told us proudly, believing in life and nature rather than an invisible realm. His face was brightened by the smile he put on for us, but his eyes were grief-stricken. His hearty, cheerful voice cracked as he spoke.

But was it sorrow or a love of freedom that motivated our hectic lifestyle? The thought suddenly popped into my head now. It made me feel green about the gills.

I felt this way often since Father pulled our cart into Pettypoole last week, the village unimportant but happy, with its pretty stone cottages and a clear, cold stream cutting through the center of it. Our lingering around it filled me with an unsettling combination of excitement and apprehension. It was far better, my father always said, to stay in a house outside town. "People can be very closed-minded, Claire. And envious. You must keep that in mind," he once said to me in an uncharacteristically dejected moment. I think I wondered even then if envy had much to do with how people viewed us. It was my father, after all, who so coveted the higher places.

I walked around the edge of the fair. There was a group of ordinary men off to the side playing cricket on a grassy clearing, some twenty onlookers applauding and shouting. Most of the men had shed their jackets, but their cheering audience kept their coats around their shoulders against the damp.

In an adjacent field, a man sheared two rare Cotswolds Lions, the honey-colored sheep native to the area. He did it at a rapid pace, his son selling the long, golden fleece in bulk to eager customers. In a pen, they kept a small herd of Dorset Horn pedigrees, Scotch half-breeds, and ordinary Cotswold Whites. That was what the sign said, at any rate.

I watched a juggler put on a show for five or six small children. They teetered unsteadily on their toddler's legs, clapping and laughing at the man. Presently, he bent gently down to them, throwing three balls, then four, then six, a colorful ring of spinning orbs.

In the center of the festival, I passed the sickly-sweet smell of the candy floss maker and could barely think for the loud bartering of several customers at a table of enormous skeins of wool dyed forest green, ox-blood red, deep navy, and chocolate brown. An acrid scent of pork fat and cheese wheels soon mixed with that of the candy floss.

The crowd, growing thicker, became swarming, engulfing. I was horribly alone in it. I thought I smelled the flesh of raw rabbit, catching a glimpse of a skinned and shiny purple carcass hanging by its feet. I stopped near a tent, my heart beating fast.

"Won't you come in a minute?"

A woman stood at the entrance to the tent. She was striking, old but not ancient, her strong nose framed by high cheekbones. Her costume was made from layers of gauzy, colorful silk. Her rather ordinary light-brown eyes were rimmed with thick coal lines. "You were here yesterday, too, weren't you?" There was, in her voice, no beckoning from a fortune-teller to a potential client, but a relaxed, unaffected greeting instead. Her hands held up the flap that was her doorway, her fingers bony and wrinkled.

"Yes," I said, first hesitating, then entering. Inside was dim and dry. There was a low table set up with thick beeswax candles, a glass globe, and a deck of tarot cards. I sat with the woman on a pile of pillows lining the floor.

"Just a month ago, I was up near York, then back down to London, then on further to Salisbury, and now here," revealed my host, a weary smile in her eyes. She let out a sigh. "You're too young for all this travel. And I'm too old."

I smiled politely, taking a cup of tea from the woman. "We've had almost the same journey," I replied.

"I know. I remember seeing you in Salisbury, at the Foxes and Dragons Festival. My name is Bella."

"I'm Claire."

"You're a pretty girl, Claire. What are you, one-and-twenty?"

"Two-and-twenty years, ma'am."

"A pretty girl indeed, but not half as noticeable as that jewel is," she said, gesturing to my neck. "That's what caught my eye. It's what made me remember you."

"My father gave it to me when I was thirteen," I said.

"Forgive me, but I'm concerned. You'd better be careful traveling as you do, on the roads. Especially at night."

I put my hand up instinctively to cover my necklace. The ring was made from thick gold, with one large ruby set into it, and was too big for any of my fingers. Father gave it to me just after we left the farm. He told me it belonged to his own father, a squire whose estate on the coast of Scotland incorporated three hundred acres of dramatic sea views and fertile land. I put the ring on a chain and had not taken it off since. I didn't know if it really belonged to my grandfather, whose person and homestead I knew only as one might know a mythic tale.

"I'm all right traveling," I said to the fortune-teller. "We seldom have trouble."

I didn't tell her that there had, in fact, been an incident. Once: a man, a dinner guest under our own roof, lecherously reached for my neck or bosom, or both. I was lying alone in bed, my sister sleeping in her own room in the vast, chilly manor house Father had rented. I awoke with a start to a large, calloused hand pulling at the shoulder of my nightdress. "C'mon then, li'l bird," said a voice in the dark, a breath raspy and sour with drink. The other hand pinned my hip down. "Lay quiet, girl, lay quiet!" The foreign, coarse skin and strong bones confined me like prey in a dog's teeth; engulfed in his stench, I screamed. The man cursed me and slipped out the door. I ran to Meg's room, pressing myself against her sleeping body under the covers. I don't know why I did not tell my father. Intoxicated himself, he slept through it all.

"My father has a way of making things work," I said, maybe a little too brightly. "We've always had fine travels."

"I think I spoke with your father yesterday," said Bella. "He directed me to the watering tent. My horses were exhausted from our journey. He looks like Father Christmas, does he not?"

I smiled. White-haired with a beard, my father did appear like a Father Christmas of sorts. He was jolly, that was true, and lucky with certain things. I would never say so, but I was beginning to suspect he was not as wise as I once thought.

"He is remarkable at finding opportunities," I said. I took a sip of my tea.

"Accommodations are another thing altogether," said Bella with a nod. "They are never good when only for a short time."

I looked at her, surprised. Though I know it was unlikely, I asked, "Can you really read minds?"

The woman laughed. "In your case, I don't have to, my dear. It's written all over your face. You look like you haven't had a good night's sleep in some time. A lumpy mattress in a drafty house will do that. Or, no, not even so luxurious a sleeping place as that?"

"No."

"Not yet, no. But the drafty house will come soon, yes?"

I meant to stay just a minute, to rest and enjoy the quiet of the tent, but Bella was kind and easy to talk to. She had some biscuits and jellies that I very much wanted, as I had only milk for breakfast. She had an honest air about her that I believed was genuine. And, for once, I did not care if it wasn't.

I soon found myself telling her about my dream: the one with Meg and the carriage. "It's a nightmare, really," I said. "I never speak of it, but I dream it anyway. And even think of it from time to time when I'm awake, as I did on Meg's wedding morning."

"Meg is your sister?"

"Yes."

"Dreams, I know," said Bella with a smile. "Dreams, I can do. Go on."

"Are you sure?"

"Tell me. How might it begin, dear?"

"I feel as if it tries to trick me. The beginning is different each time. But soon, the dream becomes the one I fear, and I find myself with my sister, the two of us walking up the High Street in a city."

"Are there cabs? Coaches?"

"There's a lot of traffic and people coming and going, but everything seems ordinary enough. Meg and I decide at some point to make our way to the other side of the city through a park. It's sparse because it's winter, though there's no snow on the ground, but I can tell it is well manicured. The air is cold, and we wear coats with fur collars, hats, and muffs like two foreigners."

Bella chuckled at this. "Like me?"

I smiled. Bella looked the part of Romany Gypsy but spoke as if she was only from Suffolk.

"How do you find yourself on the ride?" She turned more serious now.

"I don't know. We just find ourselves in a high, black barouche. The hood is open against the sky as if it's summer. There's a strong, black horse that pulls the carriage." In my mind, I could see his shoulders rotating and rippling with his gait like large swells on the sea.

"His pace grows fast," I continued. "He heads toward the park entrance, and I can hear his hoofs on the cobbled stones. The path is only meant for pedestrians, and there's a blur of people moving out of the way. I know what's going to happen next, but it's always too late. Meghan and I shout at the driver up on his coach box."

"Who is the driver?"

"I—I don't know. I can never see his face. But then we try shouting at the horse, or I try to grab the reins myself. But he has a will all his own." I thought of the horse careening recklessly along the winding path, barely missing lampposts, bare trees, and people. I couldn't bring myself to tell Bella about his splitting hoofs, the terrible splattering of blood on the path.

"Do you need some more tea, dear?"

I looked at Bella. My mouth was open and dry.

"Try to tell me what happens next," she urged in a soft voice.

"The ride lasts only a few moments more," I said. "Before I know it, the horse tears across a bridge. At the middle, he swerves and leaps over the side, taking the carriage—taking Meg and me—with him. We fall, plummeting, what seems like a long way toward the lake below. My chest feels like it's caving in, my heart left up on the bridge, my breath taken from me. Then I wake up."

We were silent for a minute. Bella crinkled her brows together, working the dream over in her mind. There was something else, too, in her face. The lighthearted sparkle that had characterized it earlier was gone.

"The horse is power," she said, putting down her teacup. "It's an ancient symbol. But what kind of power does it hold over you and your sister? Or *for* you, Claire? And who is driving the horse?"

"It's hard to tell."

"Are you *certain* there is a driver?"

"I'm not certain." I shrugged. "It frightens me in the dream."

Bella, her brows still furrowed, now looked at me with alarm.

"I'm not afraid of horses," I said quickly. "Our gelding, Johnny—or is it Teddy? Johnny was our last horse. He is quite docile."

Bella nodded, sipped her tea, then offered me more. She rubbed her chin with her forefinger, a thick, silver ring enfolding her pleated skin. "And the park, it's a large, well-tended park? As one finds in London? Or might it be more like a forest?"

"Why?"

"It's important. Observe that the next time you dream."

I did not want to observe anything the next time. I did not want to dream it again at all. "It's sparse. Like in winter. Grey and bare, exactly as I've told you." I heard my voice rising in pitch. The look of unease on Bella's face only served to make me more fearful. I disliked revealing myself to anyone I didn't know, but I thought I should give the woman anything, now, any piece of information I remembered that might help stop this.

"There are trees, and they are bare," I began again, thinking carefully. "And edged beds where flowers would be if it were spring. There are a lot of trees, even around the lake below the bridge. I've told you this!"

"There are many meanings lurking in trees: mysteries, journeys one must travel, fears one must face," Bella's voice was a hoarse whisper, a nameless dread afraid to be articulated. "And the lake, too, the one you head toward. Mystics from the East believe water is a symbol of the inner thoughts, the innermost path of one's desires and hopes and fears."

"But I always wake up when we drown."

"Ah! But do you drown? Do you actually plunge into the water?" Then she put her hands over mine: warm leather and bone strong and urging against frozen porcelain. She said slowly, "*You* know, perhaps, Claire. That is, I think, your dream knows. Maybe you're afraid to find out."

Bella poured more tea into our cups, and I drank. The tea was hot, the tent dry. The temperature had, over the last hour, grown a little milder. But I was chilled to the bone.

After the fair, my father and I headed toward the little village. The journey, though not long, stretched before me like an endless and shadowed path. It was three miles on the back of a farmer's dray; now we had sold our own cart and horse. But about a half-mile before the entrance to town, we disembarked and took the road on foot.

"The exercise will do us some good," Father said. But I knew he did not want anyone seeing him entering town on a cartload of turnips.

As the cart pulled ahead of us, I felt my own gait slow. Now it was my father's back I watched. His waistcoat had already changed, traded at the fair for one that was longer, darker. I watched the thick, fine cloth rumple with his step like the muscles on a horse.

I nearly stopped walking altogether, and he became smaller as he moved ahead of me. Looking over my shoulder, I glanced back at the winding lane as it curved through the vast open fields and pools of mud, thinning until it was just a bit of string stretching out to touch the horizon and the plain world beyond.

~ present day ~
# The Black Cat

The nights are endless up here. It's dark by three, the street lamps sparse and intermittent. More disorienting is that, though it is February in Vermont, there is not an ounce of snow on the ground.

When I pull up to the curb, it's five-thirty. With the car engine off, I hesitate a moment: one foot on the pavement, one hand on the car door. There is still the milk to get, and something sweet for later. I look down the block toward the general store, then up again.

A black bag on my shoulder gives the appearance of a simple duffel but has windows made of mesh. In it lays Pluto. His now emaciated digits grip the floor of the bag, his warm, light body snug on my hip as I stand looking at our tiny clapboard house nestled between others like it but painted in different colors: pink, yellow, barn red. The covered porches are all shadowed and bleak in the early evening pitch; devoid of Adirondacks and swings, of potted petunias. Our white one is no exception.

A sound, a rustle in the hedges from the wind, makes me think the time is much later than I thought and, perhaps, more sinister. There are all manner of unknowable things, even if they are only the lonely fairy spells and ghouls of childhood.

Peter doesn't seem to be affected by this viewpoint, and I have never tried to convince him to imagine the things that I do. Pluto as the direct descendant of gods and sorcerers when, to Peter, he is merely a cat.

"There's my girl," he says when I open the door. He's on the couch, prying off his loafer with the opposite heel. His tweed jacket is already hanging on a Shaker peg near the door, his briefcase on the floor stuffed with students' papers.

I can't deny that Peter's even-tempered, somewhat unimaginative nature is what drew me to him. That, and his tall but slightly stooped posture, the kind of confident and casual stance Ivy League graduates take after becoming keepers of the flames themselves: the possessors of knowledge and unwavering common sense. When he stood leaning on his elbow next to the lectern instead of behind it, he seemed relaxed and amiable, even as he warned us of the pitfalls of examining James and Wharton too closely, cautioning us not to read too much between the lines.

Last night, we took Pluto to the animal hospital, the vet suggesting we leave him for tests. Then we came home. I sat on the bed in my coat, staring through the little living room and to the kitchen where Peter began peeling carrots.

"It's pointless to make too much of this, Sarah," he said to the cutting board. "Are you going to take off your coat?"

"Are you even worried?"

Peter looked across the two rooms. "What's that tone for?"

"It's not a tone. It's fear."

"He's fine." Peter let the top of the garbage pail slam.

"Why? Because that would be easier?"

"Because what would be easier?"

"*It.* Me. You wouldn't have to deal with me, with my—"

Peter and I do not fight, normally; we lash out with a mordant turn of phrase, then grow quiet again. Now I felt myself attempting something greater, more hurtful, misplaced power overwhelming me and slipping from my hands like glass.

Peter said, "I thought we were talking about the cat."

Afterward, we sat on either side of the couch without Pluto, silence working its way around the room.

"Did you get him all right?" Peter cranes to peer into the mesh window now.

"Yes." I put the bag down.

"Were they okay about you leaving work early to get him?"

I nod.

He leans back on the couch and motions for me to bring the bag over. Still in my coat, hat, and gloves, I sit down and unzip it, reach in, and help him out.

A black Oriental Shorthair, Pluto is sleek and long. His tail has a break at its end, a bent line signifying aristocratic ancestry. In former times, a Mistress of the Palace would have hung a ring there and the crick in the bone would have held it in place. If the queen had died before him, he would have been slaughtered, wrapped, and buried with her as a sign of devotion. Where there once were ripples and bulky patches of muscle on Pluto, there is now just skin and dull fur. When he is not sleeping, he howls for food, yet nothing we feed him sticks.

After Peter returns from the store, we sit and watch an old movie on TV. It is *Vertigo*, and when Kim Novak comes back as the dead double, Peter lets Pluto have the melted, milky remains of a pint of ice cream. He sticks his whole narrow head into the container and wears it as a drunken party guest wears a lampshade. I can't help but laugh, and as I do, I'm hopeful. I'm certain that soon he will not be allowed to indulge in such caloric activities because soon he will be back to his weightier, hearty self, leaping from tabletops and gripping the arm of the couch with terrific agility.

We sleep with him as if he's our child, a sickly infant pressed between healthy adult bodies. At this moment, his tiny frame held against my breast is the closest I feel I will come to having a real child. I rub Pluto's ears and the top of his head, hoping good circulation will have an effect. I can feel his spine: jagged knobs under loose flesh. He is a chair frame under a leopard-skin throw. He is a Mesozoic model in a museum.

We sleep with him and wait.

The next afternoon, I walk home from work at the bookstore. The edge of my coat catches on the stiff stalk of a boxwood and, for a moment, I think something or someone has pulled on me. I know the difference between fantasy, fancy, and actuality, but sometimes it is not hard to blur the lines.

It is an unseasonably warm and rainy winter, for one thing. One season never quite gave way to the next, the two becoming one nonexistent season. I wish for snow all the time now. When Peter and I lay down at night, I imagine the silent stillness of a snowy morning and long for the deep, rasping sound of a street plow and diffused light filtering in through the window. I yearn for change.

The mountains that cradle the houses and general store are brown instead of white. The hill leading down to the store is steep and has a narrow sidewalk and large old trees and hedges lining it. In winter, it is a treacherous route, as the street is always covered in badly plowed snow and ice, the trees forming a canopy of silver, flaky, powdered diamonds and sprayed frozen white dust in our eyes and faces. But this is why we go outside in the first place. This is Narnia. These are sugarplum fairies hiding in the branches of the canopy.

Now we can walk to the store to get a loaf of bread or newspaper or sandwich, and it is no dangerous adventure to do so. The pavement is dry and the soles of my boots hold it easily. Whenever I look out the window, I can see the neighbor's house clearly. There is a planter turned upside down on the porch with a rusty hand trowel on top. The wood pile on the side of the house is not even half-gone. The grass is brown. A few drops of rain have attached themselves to our window.

In the morning, Peter stands at the kitchen sink and cracks eggs into a bowl. The bowl is very pretty, white pottery glaze with yellow and blue stripes along the edge. We bought it from a master potter in town because it reminded me of my grandmother's bread bowl, and Peter of a domesticity lurking in his family that I have only guessed at but have never actually heard directly from him. Dead when he was a boarding-school boy, his parents are a closed-lipped smile, a memory never shared.

III

"You see: it's a broad stroke when there are more than two," he says to the bowl as if it is his chalkboard, the steel gray bouncing his voice back to his rapt lecture hall as he writes. He is actually speaking to me, but we are both used to conversation this way. "Sarah, are you watching?" He cracks another egg on the side, emptying the unbroken yolk and circumfused white into it. He picks up the whisk, the largest of the two we have. He might as well be addressing an issue he had with the third page of my thesis three years ago.

"Oh, I see." I peer into the bowl because I am supposed to.

"You'd never know it," he says sharply, though he wouldn't have dared to use the tone with me when I was his student. Then he says, "Darling. I'll add another for him." He means Pluto.

"Oh, good."

I take a smaller ceramic bowl down from the shelf and begin shredding cheese into it. Holding the grater with one hand, I rub a palm-sized square hunk of Cabot cheddar across the small, sharp reliefs with the other. As I do this, I kiss the top of Pluto's head several times. He is allowed on the table. He is also allowed to dip his head into the bowl of shredded cheese.

"Why, thank you for helping," says Peter to Pluto, bending his face down but not kissing him. He's trying to be playful, though I know he thinks a cat's feet on the table is revolting. We momentarily knock against each other, Peter's rough chin and my cheek.

"Your beard is ... are you out of fresh razors?" I ask.

Peter contemplates the bowl. "No."

"I'll get some new ones."

"Maybe mine are dull," he says.

"I thought they were new. I thought I remembered to get them."

"No, they're old and dull."

I continue grating until I feel the sharp scrape of metal against my knuckle. A morsel of cheese falls to the floor. I notice there is a spot of blood on the crumble and try to think where the Band-Aids might be.

Peter looks down at the floor, takes a deep breath, exhales roughly, and looks at Pluto, who stares back at him intelligently. Peter stirs the cheese into the egg. "Did you say something, darling?" he asks.

"No. I need a Band-Aid."

"Well done, or not so, what do you think? The eggs."

"Yes. Shouldn't we wake Daniel and invite him over?" I ask, this time looking at him directly. "He'll be put out if we don't. You know how he loves an omelet."

In answer, Peter cracks another two eggs into the bowl.

Daniel is over in no time, as he lives just up the street by himself and appreciates a home-cooked breakfast. We've been neighbors since we both graduated, and I've only seen women enter or leave his house a handful of times, their relationship to him cloudy and vague. "Good morning, all. It is another brown, Global Warming day," he announces in the witty tone I am hoping for.

Throwing his coat on the sofa, he snaps his fingers as he enters the kitchen. "Sweetheart," he says, then kisses me on the forehead. "Oh, it's you," he says to Peter dryly.

"Very funny."

"Cook, I like my omelet just-so—not runny, not browned—God, that is funny," Daniel says, pointing to Pluto.

The cat has, by now, consumed at least half the amount of cheese I have grated. Daniel picks him up, sits at the table, and places him on his lap. His corduroys have bits of sawdust stuck to them, fragments from an unfinished work of art. Pluto tries to eat them.

Reaching into the cabinet above the sink, I find a Band-Aid, wrap it around my sliced knuckle, and return to my small task. While I work, I listen to Daniel trade remarks with Peter, the sound of their voices blending until they are just one voice, the voice I love to hear: it's a rapport, filled with reassurance and spirit. I look up and smile.

Daniel's black hair is sleek against the cat's as he asks Pluto, "And what do you think of all this?"

It feels like I have blinked and it's already dinner. Late morning becomes afternoon in a matter of hours, and afternoon looks more like evening than itself. It's simpler to eat two early meals, then take one long slumber. I wonder why the vet hasn't called yet.

Pluto has draped himself onto the table, his hind legs still on the chair, as he pulls a bowl of macaroni and cheese toward him.

"Hey," says Peter in a disciplinary voice, but I am laughing. "Sarah, please."

"No, no, it's very funny! Watch."

I have seen lions do this on a nature program with food items at a Serengeti campsite. The thought of this suddenly makes me feel as if what he is doing is beautiful and necessary; tragic and not comic. I pet his thin, pointed black shoulders and coax him down into his chair, the one that rests between Peter's and mine at the corner of the table.

"There's our circus cat," Peter says as he scratches under his chin. The tone of his voice, however, is layered with an irritated sigh.

I watch him watch the cat. He looks at him as if Pluto has never been his, which is not altogether untrue. He smiles good-naturedly at Pluto. He acts caring and kind to him; he would never let anyone see him behaving any other way. He lets the cat sleep with us, eat with us, and be our stand-in child; he lets me love Pluto in a way that is clearly not comfortable for him. His childhood emptiness was never filled with the wagging, truck-like insistence of dogs, the slow, hypnotic presence of cats, or even the unmemorable beauty of fish. At least this is what I am guessing, what I am imagining. I do not know the truth. Once, Peter said to me, "We didn't have dogs," but I don't know if he meant his parents, or the grandparents with whom he lived later on, or if he was referring to the fact that other people had dogs.

We eat dinner in silence. I am paralyzed, glued to my seat as Peter finishes, leaves the dishes on the table, and walks out of the room.

"Where are you going?" I whisper, unfinished dinner caught in my throat as if papier-maché. Wasps make a similar nesting material; I was taught this in elementary school by being made to chew a piece of paper until it turned to pulp.

I guess he thinks, as he so often does, that he has answered me, so he puts on his coat and goes. He heads over to Daniel's or somewhere else I am uninformed about, leaving me alone with a sob stuck in my throat that doesn't dissolve all evening.

Instead of shrugging it off and kicking my feet up in front of a movie, I sit exhausted and motionless on the couch, Pluto uncharacteristically hiding. The empty space closes in on me. Later, I get into bed. My cat is under it, and I reach for him over the edge into the space between the bed and the wall. I can hardly believe I have enough energy to do that, though somewhere in the back of my mind, I am aware that my actions are displaced.

Finally, Peter comes home. He slips under the covers and puts his arm around the cat, our arms brushing against each other.

"The test results came back positive for diabetes," the vet says. His voice, informal and relaxed, carries through the phone like someone who is reading off a list of movies playing at the local cinema.

"Wait. What?"

"I'm sorry," he says.

Stop talking, I want to say. This is not a conversation, this is a sentencing. A real one.

"Isn't it?" I say, my voice rising. I am actually getting shrill.

"Well, I don't know that I would call it a death sentence," he assures me calmly. There are routines and schedules, feeding regimens, needles, and insulin.

"He has some kidney damage, you know," the vet informs me, his voice lower, calmer.

"I did not know that."

"Some of his teeth are rotting. He may go blind. We can postpone some things."

"Like a vacation," I say sarcastically. Then, "I'm sorry." I really am sorry. "I had an uncle who had diabetes and he lived to be eighty-two," I offer.

"It's not quite the same thing. Dogs are more similar to humans, easier to manage. But not cats."

Now I wish Pluto to be a dog. *Please, just be my little, easy dog,* I think.

But he is neither human nor dog. He cannot speak or bark or perform miraculous feats of communication as though he were Rin Tin Tin. I press the vet further. I need him to tell me everything, to tell me truth instead of wishful hope. And he does.

The vet says, "Call and let me know what you decide. We'll be here through the weekend."

I touch the sharp points of Pluto's shoulders as I listen.

The vet says, "It won't be easy, either way."

Should my cat's blood-sugar level begin to fall, he tells me, he might curl up on my lap as if he were ready to be petted just like this, ready to be held and scratched behind the ears; no sign of suffering, no indication of trauma, no communication that death is suddenly quickening upon him. Perhaps, instead, he will lose his sight and will stumble fearfully even in daylight to find me.

When Pluto was born, I was there. His mother, who now resides with my aunt, pushed him out of her in one great groan, then lay still. He remained where he had landed, at her feet, cord intact and amniotic sac still internally lodged, its life-sustaining fluid uselessly trapped. His mother would not separate him, nor would she push out the sac; she remained still and apathetic, the birth itself all she felt the need to accomplish. I grasped the cord in my hands and tugged, but she had closed herself up, it seemed, and the small, black mound who would be her son, with his closed eyes and tiny claw-like paws, lay waiting to be brought into this world completely, patient as a monk.

Peter first met Pluto as most men did: by visiting my dorm room, where the cat lived in secret. In this instance, the meeting was unplanned—at two in the morning after a Modern Lit cocktail party. My cat sat on top of the dresser gazing down at us as if saying, "don't worry, your secret's safe with me," though I'm not sure how many would have really cared, with graduation being a week away. When Pluto crawled under the covers as usual, just before dawn, Peter jumped a little like a spider had moved in. "I wasn't expecting that," he said. "Neither was he," I whispered. Peter pet Pluto's head then, and that's when he said, "We didn't have dogs."

Pluto's favorite spots: on the back of the couch where the heat comes up from the baseboard and where he has a clear view of a tall tree and the neighbor's yard; on the arm of the couch where he can watch us and we can talk to him and he can beg for any food, which we willingly give over; and under the covers where we all sleep like mismatched spoons. He purrs often and easily now. I think he is happy.

I have read that recently, scientists and feline research specialists have discovered new and amazing facts about the mysterious origin and causes of the cat's purr. Yes, they say, it's true that it's a communication of the cat's own pleasure, but it is also a device used to comfort themselves when they suffer. To reassure their young, their mates, and even their human companions.

"**I**'ll build him a coffin."

Here is Daniel, our friend. My friend.

I am sitting on the couch sobbing. I notice no one has referred to Pluto by his name.

"Sarah. Sweetheart," Daniel sighs. He is promising a beautiful casket, ornate and lacquered, eighteen inches long and nine wide, a perfect fit. Daniel is a sculptor, and a good one at that.

"It's for the best," says Peter from the kitchen. "Though I'm not sure why you couldn't tell me."

"We'll give him a fine send-off," Daniel says to me. "We'll all wish we had one just like it." He holds my hand. He had dogs, growing up. I even know their names: Clyde, Henry, Jack.

"Would you like a drink?" Peter asks.

"Why not?" replies Daniel with a smile. "I see you two are ahead of me already."

I nod sheepishly. Through a vertiginous haze, I watch Peter make his way out of the kitchen with his hand on the neck of the whiskey bottle. I look around the living room for my cat, but he is under the bed again.

In the morning, we wake to the sound of church bells ringing against a silent atmosphere. A Saturday service for the devout. I reach next to me for the phone, calling the vet and alerting him of our arrival. The appointment time gives us two hours to dress and gather ourselves. We give Pluto a special breakfast, then coax him onto the couch for cartoons. Out the window, his view of the neighbor's yard is one of white, each long-awaited flake adding volume to the dusting.

I feel as if I may vomit. I feel as if I am in a nightmare in which I must convince my captors to release me before shooting me in the head, only I am the captor.

Pluto purrs incessantly. *He wants to stay,* I tell myself over and over again.

Peter looks at us both often. Searching for words, he says, "It's time to go." Nothing either of us could say on the matter would not sound monstrous at this point.

As Peter goes to the closet to get the bag, Pluto bolts, running unsteadily and dizzily into the kitchen, where he has trapped himself. I can catch him easily, and do, clutching him as if he is my child and someone evil is trying to seize him from me.

It takes us half an hour to get to the vet hospital, up winding roads, past bed and breakfasts, white churches, and barns closed against the unforgiving climate. It is snowing, finally—I can hardly believe it—and the roads are icy. The frost that has worked its way into the ground since midnight is working its way in through the windows. The windshield wipers squeak in rhythm.

Peter is silent. He looks angry, as if I have done or said something inappropriate. We are about to fight. But what are we fighting over? We are just taking a drive. This is what I am supposed to say to my cat. Our cat.

We are just taking a drive. I am to deceive him as much as possible. But I can't speak. I can't even speak when we arrive, when he is placed on the examining table and given a sedative injection. I kneel before the steel table, wanting him on my lap. I only say, "Pluto, Pluto. Look at me, look at me, look at me!" because now he is closing his eyes but breathing hard and labored, fighting the sedative. I hear Peter say to the receptionist in the hall, "May we have a glass of water, please?" He gives me the water, and when I turn to look at him, he is in a chair, crying.

After it is over, we place him in Daniel's lacquered box and get back in the car.

What a thing I've done. God, what a thing I've just done.

"Are you asleep yet?"

"No, not yet." I try to find Peter's hand in the dark. There is a cold spot between us where the sheets are still covered in fur.

"We gave him some very happy years."

"Yes," I say, though it has not been so many for Peter.

"And Daniel did a nice job. That was some send-off." I sense Peter smiling sadly.

The burial itself was more difficult than any of us imagined. The ground was tough and unyielding; Peter broke a sweat in his wool coat. There was the root of a tree, and another try digging some inches over. In a nod to wintry misfortune and a Gothic aesthetic, Daniel had affixed a carved mahogany cross to the lid of Pluto's coffin; tiny roses and thorns in relief under my fingertips I did not want to release. They were covered in earth first with fists, then shovels, until there was only a mound the size of a newborn child left beneath the tree.

In the morning, Daniel arrives with doughnuts and the Sunday paper. "Good morning, all! It is a glorious day. The trees look like candied sugar, and the hill is officially deadly to walk down."

"Ah, coffee." Peter peers into the brown paper bag. "And to think of the risk you took to bring us such a breakfast treat."

"It was worth it just to see your hair."

"I work very hard at my hair."

"Is he always this humble?" Daniel says to me. "Smells great. Hand me one of those things."

"Can you hand me my cup?" I ask. "Did you put sugar in it?"

"Of course."

Looking out the window, Peter examines the coated street below. "Well, it certainly snowed yesterday. Would you hand me a doughnut? No, the cinnamon kind."

"Don't you think it's strange? The snow, I mean," Daniel comments seriously as he breaks a piece of sugar doughnut and dips it in his coffee. "It hasn't felt like winter up until now. All that warm rain, and then just yesterday. Well ..." He looks uncomfortably at me.

I follow Daniel's gaze to the window, the street below, and the frozen grass lying under thick white. "Yes, it snowed a great deal yesterday," I say.

"Well."

"It'll be frozen solid through now," I say.

"What will, darling?" Peter's mouth is full of cake and coffee as he reaches across me for a napkin.

"I think she means—"

"Yes, frozen through," I say again.

There is a moment of thought on the matter. When Peter has swallowed the last of his coffee with an enthusiastic gulp, he smacks his lips and wrinkles his brows. "How 'bout a walk?"

"Good idea," Daniel agrees.

"Oh, I don't know," I say, my voice tired.

"No, I'd love to visit him."

"Would you?" I reach out and put my hand on Daniel's arm.

Peter agrees. "Let's all get our coats, shall we?"

Down the hill, we slip and slide, knocking into each other playfully, grasping at a fence or signpost for balance. Narnia has appeared beyond the wardrobe. The ice crinkles like glass crystals around us. I can't feel my nose. Daniel says something funny and, laughing as one for just a moment, we are suddenly all on the ground, piled into a drift. McKenzie's Tow Service truck honks its horn at us and we wave.

Soon, we're up another hill that leads to the forest and, blindly choosing what looks like a path, we head in.

The only marker is a small, wood plaque that we nailed to a tree yesterday. Below it, the ground is flattened out in a rare and newly tamped way. It has taken us a while to find it since everything in the forest resembles itself. Yesterday, the woods echoed with the chopping sound of shovels breaking ground. Today, we can barely hear each other in the white, muffled landscape.

"Let's join hands," Daniel suggests.

"I'm not one for prayer," says Peter.

"Let's just be silent, then. Let's just be here."

I feel Daniel's hand and Peter's hand, in mine. I close my eyes and bow my head. I feel a hand tug on mine—I don't know whose—urging me to sit as though in a spiritual gathering or nursery-school game.

We hold hands and slowly lower ourselves to the ground. It is not snow-covered on the grave, but smoothed out with soil, devoid of stones or twigs, as if all in nature has avoided it. I find myself lying stomach-down on the ground, my head turned to Peter. We are in a flat circle, as if we are worshipers of some nature cult or lying down for a poison-induced sleep. Our breathing becomes synchronized. I close my eyes, my cheek flat against the ground, my ear to the clear, hard earth.

My eyes are closed, and when I hear a heartbeat, they fly open. Then silence. I hear it again. No, it's mine.

"Can you hear that?" I whisper.

"Yes," says Peter. "It's nothing. Just us."

"Where are you going?"

"Let's go for a walk. Come on." Peter is getting up now, helping Daniel up, too.

"Wait a minute ... listen." My ear is still to the ground. My breathing and pulse sound echoed and elongated. It's fascinating, and I can't bring myself to leave it. Then, among the pulses and wind-tunnel gusts of breath, there is a rustling sound. It is coming from under the surface.

It's just my own breath, I tell myself. But even so, I feel terrified. I hear it again. The sound is coming from directly below me. Rustling, then a scratch or two, then more.

"Don't you hear it?" I ask. No one answers. Without lifting my head, I try looking near and above me. They are already gone; I'm alone here on the ground.

There is another scratch. I jump up from the ground, the damp earth stuck to my face like plaster.

"Peter! Peter!"

I am bolting through the woods, backtracking over my own footsteps; branches, like taut metal springs, snap painfully against my neck and shoulder.

"Peter, wait for me. Wait!"

Everywhere is white, white with gray and black bare trees. I slow down, thinking I'm just spooking myself. Even so, my heart is racing and I feel my eyes sting with tears. I look around the woods calling for Daniel and Peter and, when I can't find them, I decide the best thing to do is go home. They are probably way ahead of me by now, anyway. They walk briskly and have longer legs than I do. My heart is beating hard inside my chest. I'm out of breath. Yes, by now they're home, a trick meant to scare me, then make me laugh.

I walk back up the slippery, dangerous hill to meet them.

When I walk through the door, it is very warm inside. Warm and bright—the light is filtering through the clouds and working its way past the window panes. Lovely.

"Peter?"

No one is home. I look in the kitchen, the little room in the back I use for a study, and the bedroom. Back in the living room again. There is no one. No one but Pluto, who sits, perfectly and neatly tucked, on the couch.

For a moment, all I can think of is that I can't believe I didn't notice him before. He is in the middle of one of the cushions, not his favorite spot on the arm. I move slowly across the room to him.

"My ..." I whisper. "What ..." And finally, stupidly, "What are you doing here?"

I kneel down before him. He looks at me with cloudy eyes, the eyes of cataracts and ulcers, of cadavers. Above one rests a tiny lump of dirt. The fur of his rump, too, is dulled by a streak of loam. I go to pet him. I can barely bring myself to touch his cold body, the sharp bones of his spine. The dull, lifeless fur.

"There's still time," I whisper, petting him gently. I feel tears of terror, of longing, welling up in my eyes again, my vision blurry like a gift; I cannot stand the sight of my dead cat sitting in my house.

"We've been given a second chance," I hear myself say into the ground, my hand clutching Peter's. But he doesn't answer me. His fingers begin to pry themselves from mine. "We should take it. It's a second chance." I wait for an answer; I am not the one deciding this time. It's also Peter's choice now.

At the same time, in the living room, I kneel at the couch and stroke my beloved cat's head—the part of his fur that's still good and velvety, behind the ear. I talk in a low, sweet voice. I comfort him; I stroke his skeletal back. When he looks at me, it is with empty, zombie eyes.

What a thing I have been doing.

When Peter finally comes home, I'm in the bedroom packing.

"Where did you go? You ran off," he says. Then he says, "Where are you going?"

I press four pairs of underwear into Pluto's black duffel bag. Four will be enough. Before four days have passed, I will be north of here to where it has been snowing for weeks.

"Darling?" Peter takes a step toward me, then backs up again, setting his mouth tightly. He sits on the couch. It doesn't take him long before he says, "Where should I send your other things?"

But I am out the door, the duffel over my shoulder, its mesh window lying lightly against my back. A truck whooshes by on the slush-covered, black street and makes a sound like a hose being turned on to water a lawn or wash a car.

As I stand with the car door still open, a drop of rain hits my lip. I stop and look up at the sky. I think about the grave we have made and the frozen earth that will now settle and sink with rain, running off onto the forest floor, the tip of the coffin perhaps unveiled.

It doesn't matter, I tell myself. He was never ours. He was never mine.

~ Author's Notes ~

I am very grateful to Kathryn Tarlow Sears and Lesléa Newman for being thorough, detailed, and understanding editors. I am also thankful for the editing and reading skills of Erin O'Donnell, Jennifer Winters, and Richard and Gail Gambino. Thank you, as well, to Emily Kitschell and Hilary Thayer Hamann, whose knowledge and understanding of the process of writing, and the business of publishing, helped me tremendously. To Alexander, Liam, and Beatrix: I owe thanks for making life unimaginably better than it was before you were in it.

    The main characters and plots of the stories in this collection are fictitious. That said, certain aspects are based on or inspired by true facts or events. "Dog Boy," for example, was inspired in part by an actual canine tracking program, which went amiss at a Texas penitentiary, in 1991.

    Nanette, in "Forever Jim," grew as a character from a real woman I encountered while photographing Père Lachaise Cemetery in Paris, where scrawled graffiti and evidence of vandals really do lead to Jim Morrison's grave.

    The farm where Anja lives in "Counting Sheep" still exists in a different form in Bridgehampton, New York. The incident of the German men visiting Dr. Vonlinden is based on the following true occurrence: on June 13, 1942, four men landed on a beach near Amagansett, Long Island, just after midnight. They came from a German submarine bringing with them explosives in an attempt to sabotage the manufacturing of equipment and supplies needed on the battlegrounds of Europe. The saboteurs were arrested, tried before a military commission, and found guilty, several receiving the death penalty.

As for the Great Hurricane of 1938, on which the storm in "Counting Sheep" was based, it was the first major hurricane to strike the New England coastline since 1869 and remains, to date, the most powerful, costliest, and deadliest hurricane in New England history. The steeple of the Old Whaler's Church in Sag Harbor, ripped down by the high winds, has still not been replaced.

"The Dream" is the first chapter in the novel *The Crewel Wing*. While the areas and counties described in it are real, the village of Pettypoole is not; the characters, likewise, are fictitious.

ABOUT THE AUTHOR

Erica-Lynn Huberty graduated from New York University, and holds an M.A. in literature and visual arts from Bennington College. Her fiction, poetry, and essays have been anthologized in over seven collections including *Garrison Keillor: Good Poems*. Her articles have appeared in The Washington Post, The New York Times, and Sculpture magazine, among other publications. She lives on Eastern Long Island with her husband and children.

Made in the USA
Lexington, KY
13 July 2010